John Fitch

The Original Steam-Boat Supported

Or, a reply to Mr. James Rumsey's pamphlet. Shewing the true priority of

John Fitch, and the false datings, &c. of James Rumsey

John Fitch

The Original Steam-Boat Supported
Or, a reply to Mr. James Rumsey's pamphlet. Shewing the true priority of John Fitch, and the false datings, &c. of James Rumsey

ISBN/EAN: 9783337413255

Printed in Europe, USA, Canada, Australia, Japan

Cover: Foto ©Andreas Hilbeck / pixelio.de

More available books at **www.hansebooks.com**

THE
ORIGINAL
STEAM-BOAT

SUPPORTED;

OR,

A REPLY

TO

Mr. JAMES RUMSEY's PAMPHLET.

SHEWING THE

TRUE PRIORITY

OF

JOHN FITCH,

AND THE

FALSE DATINGS, &c.

OF

JAMES RUMSEY.

PHILADELPHIA:

PRINTED BY ZACHARIAH POULSON, JUN^R. ON THE
WEST SIDE OF FOURTH-STREET, BETWEEN
MARKET AND ARCH-STREETS,
M DCC LXXXVIII.

PREFACE.

AGREEABLY to a promise made in the Independant Gazetteer, I now present to the Public a reply to the Pamphlet published by Mr. Rumsey, of Virginia,—and as I have no matter to conceal, or disguise, and wish my Readers to have a full and fair view of the whole controversy, I have reprinted and annexed Mr. Rumsey's Pamphlet, which will discover, to every impartial person who will take the trouble to examine the subject, that he hath no sort of just pretension to the claims he hath exhibited.—His skill in the mechanism of a Steam Engine, may possibly be greater than mine, and in the article of CONDENSATION I freely acknowledge he is my superior, having acquired the art of *condensing* (with the dash of his pen) one *whole year* into the compass of *six days.*

JOHN FITCH.

Philadelphia, 10th. May, 1788.

"HONOR TO WHOM HONOR IS DUE"
ORIGIN OF STEAM NAVIGATION.
A VIEW OF COLLECT POND AND ITS VICINITY
in the City of New York in 1803

BY JOHN HUTCHINGS

John Fitch's First Boat Perseverance

REMARKS

DESCRIPTION

Scene of the City of New York Portrait

THE WORLD IS INDEBTED FOR THE ORIGINAL IDEA AND TO THE MECHANICAL GENIUS OF JOHN FITCH, OF EAST WINDSOR, CONN.

And to the perseverance and indefatigable attention to the use of Steam of Robert Fulton Esq. The wealth & exalted character of Robert R. Livingston Esq. Chancellor of the State of New York.

Entered according to act of Congress in the year 1846 by JOHN HUTCHINGS in the Clerk's Office of the District Court of the Southern District of N.Y.

THE

ORIGINAL

STEAM-BOAT

SUPPORTED, &c.

IT is the duty of every man not only to avoid the commiſſion of a crime, but ſo to conduct himſelf through life as to bear the ſtricteſt ſcrutiny.

In a Pamphlet publiſhed by Mr. James Rumſey and lately circulated in this City, as well as probably in other ſtates, I am charged as the perpetrator of crimes attrocious in their nature, but of which my conſcience fully acquits me. It is an exerciſe of malevolence in the extreme thus publicly to prefer charges againſt an innocent perſon without previouſly knowing or enquiring for the defence of the ſuppoſed offender, and ſhews an inability in the accuſer to ſupport his charges. Unfortunately for Mr. Rumſey, I truſt we are now before an impartial Public; where Juſtice, unbiaſſed by party or undue influence, will decide between us—Concious of my conduct, in the proſecution of this buſineſs, being that of an honeſt man, it is incumbent on me to recite the circumſtances, and facts relative thereto.

I confeſs the thought of a Steam-boat, which firſt ſtruck me by mere accident, about the middle of April 1785,* has hitherto been very unfortunate to me; the perplexities and embarraſſments through which it has cauſed me to wade, far exceed any thing, that the common courſe of life ever preſented to my view. After pondering ſome days on the thought, I made a rough draught, but not daring to truſt my own opinion too far, I conſulted Mr. Daniel Longſtreth, the Reverend Nathaniel Irvin and ſundry other Gentlemen of Bucks county, Pennſylvania.

About the beginning of June, 1785, I went to Philadelphia and ſhewed it to Dr. Ewing, Mr. Patterſon and other reſpectable characters in the city, from whom I met with no diſcouragement. In June and July I formed models and in Auguſt laid them before Congreſs, as will appear on their Files. In September

* Vide Nᵒ· 1 and 2

tember I prefented them to the Philofophical Society, as per certificate

N°. 3.

Philadelphia, 1785.

September 27th. 1785. At a fpecial meeting of the American Philofophical Society:

A Model, accompanied with a drawing and defcription of a machine for working a boat, againft the ftream, by means of a Steam Engine, was laid before the fociety by JOHN FITCH.

At a meeting of the American Philofophical Society, on December 2d. 1785.

A Copy of the drawing and defcription of a machine for working a boat againft the current, which, fome time ago, was laid before the fociety by Mr. JOHN FITCH, he, this evening, *prefented* to them.

Extract from the Minutes,

SAMUEL MAGAW,

One of the Secretaries.

In October I called on the ingenious Mr. Henry, of Lancafter, to take his opinion of my drafts, who informed me, that I was not the firft perfon who had thought of applying Steam to veffels; that he had converfed with Mr. Andrew Ellicott as early as the year 1775, and that Mr. Paine, author of Common Senfe, had fuggefted the fame thing to him in the winter of 1778; that fome time after, he (Mr. Henry) thinking more ferioufly of the matter, was of opinion it might be eafily perfected and accordingly made fome drafts which he propofed to lay before the Philofophical Society and which he then fhewed me, but added as he had neglected to bring them to public view, and as I had firft publifhed the plan to the world, he would lay no claim to the invention. The following I have been favoured with from Mr. Ellicott:

N°. 4.

Baltimore, April 26th. 1787.

I do hereby certify, that early in the year one thoufand, feven hundred and feventy five, Mr. William Henry, of Lancafter, converfed with me on the fubject of *fteam,* and intimated that he thought it might be advantageoufly applied to the Navigation of Boats.

(Signed)

ANDREW ELLICOTT.*

From Lancafter I went to the Affembly of Virginia, firft waiting on Governor Johnfon, of Maryland, who, notwithftanding the letters he has fince written in favour of Mr. Rumfey, acknowledged a merit in my invention and that it ought to be encouraged,

* *Vide Mrs. Henry's Certificate* N°. 5.

couraged, as will prefently appear. During my journey through Maryland, in October, I paffed through Frederick Town, and every where publifhed my Plan. In Virginia I waited on his Excellency General Wafhington, who, in the courfe of converfation, informed me, that the thought of applying Steam was not original, that Mr. Rumfey had mentioned Steam to him; but nothing that paffed in the converfation with General Wafhington had the leaft tendency to convey the idea of Mr. Rumfey's relying on Steam, and General Wafhington's letter, page 10, in Mr. Rumfey's pamphlet, clears up the matter—for the General himfelf did not conceive any fuch thing. Knowing that the thought of applying Steam to Boats had been fuggefted by other gentlemen *long before*, I left his Excellency General Wafhington with all the elated profpects that an afpiring projector could entertain, not doubting but I fhould reap the full benefit of the project, for although I found that *fome* had *conceived* the thought before, yet I was the firft that ever exhibited a plan to the public; and was fully convinced that I could not interfere with Mr. Rumfey, otherwife the known candor of General Wafhington muft have pointed out to me fuch interference. I immediately applied to the Legiflature of Virginia for affiftance, to execute my plan, who fignified their wifh to encourage my defigns, but that the ftate of their finances prevented it—the then Governor of the ftate, Patrick Henry, Efq. received from me an obligation with provifion, that if I procured in that ftate a fale for one thoufand of my Maps of the N. W. part of the United States, at 6/8 each, I fhould exhibit a Steam Boat on the waters of Virginia, within nine months or forfeit and pay to the ftate of Virginia, £ 350. as appears by the following certificate:

No. 6.

I certify, that John Fitch has left in my hands a bond payable to the Governor for the time being for £ 350, conditioned for exhibiting his fteam Boat when he receives fubfcriptions for 1000 of his maps, 6/8 each.

November 16th. 1785.
(Signed)

P. HENRY.

I then returned to Maryland and acquainted Governor Johnfon of my expected affiftance in Virginia and that I intended applying to the Affembly of Maryland then fitting, to promote and patronize my fcheme—Governor Johnfon gave me the following Letter to General Smallwood, the then Governor of the ftate.

No. 7.

SIR,   *Frederick Town, November* 25, 1785.
Mr. John Fitch of Bucks county, in Pennfylvania, called on me in his way to Richmond; he has gone through a variety of fcenes

in

in the back country, which has enabled him to collect a knowledge of a great part of the new states, on which and other
helps he has made a map useful and entertaining; his ingenuity
in this way strongly recommends him, but his genius is not confined to this alone, he has spent much thought on an improvement of the Steam-engine, by which to gain a first power applicable to a variety of uses, amongst others to force vessels forward
in any kind of water; if this engine can be simplified, constructed
and made to work at a small expence, there is no doubt but it
will be very useful in most great works, and amongst them in
ship building. Mr. Fitch wants to raise money to make an experiment on Boats, the countenance that he has met with in Virginia
he hopes will enable him to do it, he wishes also to make other
experiments, and is willing to enter into engagements to apply
a large proportion of the sales of his maps, his principle fund.
I believe his passion for this improvement will be ample security
for his applying the money in that way;—all that I have to request
of you Sir, is, that you will give him an opportunitiy to converse
with you, you will soon perceive he is a man of real genius and
modesty, your countenancing him will follow of course.

I am Sir,

your Excellency's

most obedient and most humble Servant,

(Subscribed)   THOS. JOHNSON,.

His Excellency Governor Smallwood.

Favour of

Mr. Fitch.

From hence it plainly appears, that Governor Johnson could
not at that time have any idea of my scheme interfering with
Mr. Rumsey's, as seems to be now insinuated in that gentleman's
letter to Mr. Rumsey, N°. 14 of his Pamphlet.

I attended the session of the legislature about three weeks after
receiving this letter, and on my petition for assistance to execute
my plan, they made me the following report or nearly in these
words, (as may appear by examining their minutes) " However
desirous it is for liberal and enlightened legislatures to encourage
useful arts, yet the state and condition of our finances are such
that there can be no advance of public money at present."
From this report it is proved beyond all doubt, that the Assembly of Maryland did not conceive my plan the same as Mr. Rumsey's—finding that I was undoubtedly the first person in America that could be termed the inventor of a Steam Boat, either
agreeably to custom, or equity, I thought it prudent to apply to
the different states for the exclusive privileges for the emoluments of such invention, which were granted by New-Jersey in
March 1786, by Delaware, New York and Pennsylvania in the
winter and spring following, and by Virginia in October, 1787.

I have

I have from the time of my firſt thought purſued my ſchemɞ with unremitted application, without a ſuſpicion of an interruption, until the circulation of Mr. Rumſey's invidious Pamphlets, the contents of which I now find it neceſſary next to take under conſideration, not doubting but that the deſign and tendency of that production will be a ſufficient apology for the plainneſs with which I ſhall treat it.

Mr Rumſey ſays in page 2, " That in the month of September, 1784, he exhibited the model of a Boat to his Excellency General Waſhington, at Bath, in Berkeley County, calculated for ſtemming the current of *rapid rivers only*, conſtructed on principles very different from (his) preſent one; ſatisfied of the experiment of her making way againſt a rapid ſtream by *the force of the ſtream*, the General was pleaſed to give me a moſt ample certificate of her efficacy." Here it is to be obſerved, that no mention was made to General Waſhington of *ſteam*, at the time of ſuch exhibition; the principles upon which the Boat was propelled, were entirely unconnected with, and diſtinct from, ſteam; being ſimply a model, propelled by water wheels, cranks and ſetting poles; a mode which was many years ago tried on the river Schuylkill by a farmer near Reading, but without ſucceſs. From an exhibition of this plan it was that Mr. Rumſey procured the certificate from General Waſhington, and on that certificate were Mr. Rumſey's laws founded. In his petitions to the ſeveral legiſlatures, he prayed for no excluſive right, for the uſe of Steam Boats; neither did he make mention of Steam, to their committees; or even ſuggeſt an idea of the kind: as proof of which, I offer the following petition to the Aſſembly of Pennſylvania, the certificate from General Waſhington, accompanying it, and the certificate of Manuel Eyre, Eſquire, who was one of the committee of Aſſembly, who reported in Mr. Rumſey's favor.

N°. 8.

I have ſeen the model of Mr. Rumſey's Boats, conſtructed to work againſt ſtreams; examined the powers upon which it acts, been eye witneſs to an actual experiment, in running water of ſome rapidity; and give it as my opinion (although I had little faith before) that he has diſcovered the art of working Boats by mechaniſm and ſmall manual aſſiſtance againſt rapid currents; that the diſcovery is of vaſt importance; may be of the greateſt uſefulneſs in our inland navigation, and, if it ſucceeds, of which I have no doubt, that the value of it is greatly enhanced by the ſimplicity of the works, which when ſeen and explained, may be executed by the moſt common mechanic.

Given under my hand, at the Town of Bath, County of Berkeley, in the State of Virginia, this 7th. of September, 1784.

GEORGE WASHINGTON.

N°. 9.

N°· 9.

To the Honourable the Representatives of the State of Pennsylvania,
in General Assembly met.

GENTLEMEN,

Whereas your petitioner has formed a plan for facilitating the navigation of rapid rivers; he therefore doth propose to construct a certain species of Boats of the burthen of ten tons which shall sail or be propelled by the combined influence of certain mechanical powers thereto applied, the distance of between twenty-five and forty miles per day, against the current of a rapid river, notwithstanding the velocity of the water should move at the rate of five miles per hour and upwards, with the burthen of ten tons on board, to be wrought at no greater expence than that of three hands; and as a premium of so useful an invention, your petitioner prays for an act to pass this honourable house, granting to your petitioner, his heirs and assigns, the sole and exclusive right of constructing, navigating and employing boats constructed upon his new invented-model upon each and every creek, river, bay, inlet and harbour within the limits and jurisdiction of this commonwealth, for and during the term of ten years, fully to be compleated and ended, to be computed from the first day of January next; provided always, that the legislature of this commonwealth may, at any time within the term aforesaid, abolish the exclusive right herein prayed for, by the payment of ————— pounds in gold or silver. And your petitioner, as in duty bound, shall pray.

JAMES RUMSEY.

The foregoing is a true copy of the original petition remaining on the files of the General Assembly and read in the house November 26, 1784.

J. SHALLUS, *Ast. Clk.*

N°· 10.

Philadelphia, the 6th. May, 1788.

This may certify, that I the subscriber was in Assembly for the year 1784, and was appointed one of the committee to report on Mr. James Rumsey's petition for his Boat to go against the streams of rapid rivers, and that there was no mention nor any idea held up to the committee that it was to be propelled by the force of steam.

(Signed)

MANUEL EYRE.

Now I ask, whether it does not amount to a positive proof that Mr. Rumsey had no sort of reference to, or dependance on, Steam? General Washington says, " It is so *simple* that it may be executed by the most *common mechanic;*" which certainly his Excellency

cellency would not have faid of a Steam-engine; a machine, that has coft me two years to underftand, and compleat. If we examine the Petition, we fhall find, that it confirms the General's idea of fimplicity; for Mr. Rumfey fays " it may be wrought at no *greater expence* than that of *three* hands," plainly indicating, that the *expence of fire* was not in contemplation; and to put the matter out of all doubt, Mr. Eyre declares, " *There was no idea* held up to the committee that it was to be propelled by *Steam.*"

All Mr. Rumfey's laws were obtained, in confequence of his model, fhown to General Wafhington at Bath; which, as I have faid, was nothing but water wheels, cranks and fetting poles; therefore he could have no pretenfion to the ufe of Steam, under thofe laws. With the fame propriety, his claim might extend to every power, and every machine in the United States; as foon as any man had invented one that would fuit his purpofe. So that upon his plan of law making, no other man would be fafe in expending his money, but all muft be fwallowed up by his pretendedly ambiguous laws. But I am happy in knowing, that *his laws*, as well as *his claims*, cannot interfere with *mine*; for had he profeffed any reliance on Steam; or any intention to apply it to his boats, he certainly would not have neglected inferting, fo important a part of the fcheme, in his petitions to the different legiflatures. Nor would he have prayed to be invefted with the exclufive privilege, to ufe boats, conftructed on fuch different principles from thofe he really intended to purfue. In Mr. Rumfey's act paffed in Pennfylvania, it is ftiled " The exclufive right of conftructing, navigating and employing boats built and to be built on his new invented mode," and this new invented mode (viz. cranks, water wheels and fetting poles) is all he was entitled to under that law. Can it be fuppofed that the legiflatures would not have included Steam in their laws, if they had been informed by Mr. Rumfey that it was his grand dependance; the effential, the vital part of his fcheme, as he now profeffes. That they had no fuch intimation given them, is very evident, from their encouragement to me; and the laws fince paffed, are the fulleft proofs of the received meaning of Mr. Rumfeys petitions, viz. that they had no connection with Steam. And that Mr. Rumfey did not think himfelf mifunderftood, muft certainly be granted; becaufe he made no objection to any of my petitions, as interfering with his Laws, which, agreeable to his own declarations, were founded on principles very different from a Steam-boat. That he had no claim to Steam under his laws is evident, from his confeffion in page 4, line 31, where he fays " I find my idea of Steam was *nearly matured* before fteam had ever entered his head by his confeffion to Governor Johnfon viz. April 1785."—Now can it be fuppofed Mr. Rumfey had made confiderable *improvements* on Steam-engines in 1784, or

that

that he had obtained laws fecuring a right to the ufe of Steam to Boats, when at the time of his petitioning for, and the paffing of thofe laws, he confeffes his idea of Steam was not *matured*.

He fays in page 3, line 1, " In the courfe of that fall and winter of 1784, he made progrefs in fome Steam-engines, and page 16, line 7, of Governor Johnfon's letter, " I think in October 1785, you told me you relied on Steam for your firft power, and wifhed me to promote your having fome cylinders caft at my brother's and my works; the attempt did not fucceed." Speaking of General Wafhington, the Governor adds " But the General feems to have thought it an *immatured idea that he did not imagine you then relyed on*" (viz. in November 1784.) Thefe two laft acknowledgements on the part of Mr. Rumfey, muft deftroy the facts alledged in the firft, viz. that " He made progrefs in Steam-engines in the fall and winter of 1784." For the information given to General Wafhington in confidence refpecting the boat, was fuch that the General " Did not think he then relyed on Steam;" which is fully confirmed, by his making ufe of the General's certificate to the Affemblies, wherein the difcovery is treated as being " enhanced by its fimplicity, and may be executed by the moft common mechanic" which furely no perfon would fay of a Steam-engine.

His application to Governor Johnfon for caftings for a Steam-engine, is infinuated to have been in October or November 1785, which I muft deny, and refer to the Governor's own letter for the proof; being confident that no fuch application had been made to that gentleman by Mr. Rumfey, *previous* to my obtaining the letter of Recommendation to Governor Smallwood. But even had it been true it goes no further back than October or November 1785, which was the very time I was publifhing my plan through Pennfylvania, Maryland and Virginia, and was near three months after the time I laid it before Congrefs—And yet this attempt to have a cylinder caft, at Governor Johnfon's works in October or November 1785, is the firft effay towards bringing forward a Steam-engine, that is offered in proof, admitting it to have been at the time Governor Johnfon fuppofes, which I cannot allow for reafons I fhall prefently offer in addition to what I have already faid on this head. Then how are we to reconcile the affertion of Mr. Rumfey's having made confiderable progrefs in Steam-engines in the " fall or winter of 1784," when it appears his firft attempt (by this account) was not made until after October or November 1785 as mentioned by Governor Johnfon's letter. I fhall hereafter fhow, to a demonftration, beyond all poffibility of doubt, that this fame engine, faid to have been compleatly made in Frederick town in December 1785, *was not begun* until March 1786. On comparing Governor Johnfon's letter, fent under my care to General Smallwood, dated November 25th. 1785, (a confiderable time after I firft explained to him my model

del

del and acquainted him of my intentions of pursuing the scheme) with his letter to Mr. Rumsey, dated December the 18th. 1787, it must unavoidably call in question the *memory* or *candour* of the writer, the *latter* I most certainly ought to acquit, and should have been happy had I obtained the least *explanation* on this head, when I lately made a journey to his house; expressly to procure it; possibly it may still be received. If Governor Johnson knew, and believed the legal priority of Mr. Rumsey's claim, to a Steam-boat, and was entrusted with his secret, how was it possible he could have encouraged a man " *of real genius and modesty*" (as he was pleased to term me) to proceed on an experiment, which terminate as it would, must inevitably end in loss and disappointment. For should the experiment fail, which was then thought very doubtful, the small fund, which I should raise by the sale of my maps, must likewise fail; for I was to expend it in Virginia as appears by Governor Henry's certificate page 5. Should the experiment succeed to the utmost of my wishes, I should suffer more severely, not in my money and time only, but in my reputation; and meet the treatment of a man trespassing on the rights of a fellow citizen, who had a law in his favour. Had Governor Johnson at the time he encouraged me, known the priority of claim to be fairly and justly in Mr. Rumsey, had he been *then* in possession of his secret, or had he believed any title vested in Mr. Rumsey to the exclusive use of Steam, under the law of Maryland, so recently passed in his favor, the Governor certainly would not have requested a gentleman of General Smallwood's rank, to countenance me, not only to trespass on the rights of Mr. Rumsey, but to violate a law, which as Governor of the state he was bound to support. Another circumstance corroborates my assertion of misrelation of facts, as to time.

It will be recollected that Governor Johnson's letter recommending me so very minutely and warmly to the patronage of Governor Smallwood, was dated 25th. November 1785, and in his letter to Mr. Rumsey, the Governor says, " In October or November 1785, you told me you relied on Steam for your first power and wished me to promote your having some castings at my brother's and my works; the attempt did not succeed—I considered myself under an obligation to secresy, 'till in the progress of making copper cylinders in Frederick Town, *some time after*, when I found that the designed purpose of the cylinder was a *subject of pretty general conversation*."—Now the Governor's letter in my favour was dated 25th. November 1785, and the whole machinery is sworn to have been compleated on the 1st. December following, only six days after the time of my getting this letter of recommendation—and as the cylinder was a subject of " pretty general conversation," I could not have been kept in ignorance by the Governor from his " Obligation to secresy" because it was no longer a secret at Frederick-town.

The

The thing was impoffible in its nature, that the cylinders and
copper works fhould have been making, and a fubject of general
converfation, in Frederick-town, on the 25th. day of November
1785, the time I was obtaining my letter of introduction to Governor Smallwood, in that very town; and muft have heard it
myfelf, if Governor Johnfon had been fo difingenuous as to conceal it from me; which is abfurd to fuppofe; for I made my bufinefs publicly known in that town, and therefore, if Mr. Rumfey's cylinders were the fubject of general converfation, I muft
have heard it from every quarter; therefore it clearly follows,
that the converfation about cafting of the cylinders, the obligation of fecrefy, and the general converfation about the
defign of the cylinders in Frederick-town, could not have happened in the year 1785.—If Mr. Rumfey had made Governor
Johnfon his confident " In October or November 1785,"
it is highly improbable that he would fo far have deceived
Mr. Rumfey and me, as to encourage my purfuit of a fimilar
nature, within fo fhort a time as fix days of its being compleated.
—And it is equally improbable that Mr. Rumfey fhould have
communicated this fecret and requefted his affiftance in procuring caftings immediately after my being with the Governor, as
there was not time for it—the Engine being fworn as I have faid
to have been all compleated fix days after that vifit—Then the
following conclufion may be fafely drawn, that Governor Johnfon did at fome fubfequent day (fo long after as that he forgot the
letter he had given me) offer to affift Mr. Rumfey with caftings:
which not fucceeding, an application was made to copperfmiths
in Frederick-town the enfuing fpring, who in the courfe of the
fummer 1786, delivered their work to Mr. Rumfey.—About this
time it was that the matter became a fubject of " general converfation"—and if winter ftopped the putting the whole machinery
into motion as fworn to by Meffrs. Barns and Morrow, it was the
winter of 1786, which is long after my boat was built, and my
model of a Steam engine compleated.—Of this my readers will
foon be fully convinced—and a further weighty proof is—that
as Mr. Rumfey profeffes his hurrying on his engine, was on account of my fetting up pretenfions, it cannot be believed that he
would fuffer my petition to lay before the affembly of Maryland,
and be reported on in my favour about the 20th. December 1785,
nineteen days after he fays his boat and Engine were finifhed—Mr.
Foy the member from Frederick-town muft have told the tale,
and laid in a claim for his countryman,—but I repeat it again,
that I was in that very Frederick-town on my way to the Affembly in the fall of 1785, every where publifhing my fcheme, and no
Engine was begun there during that year, nor until March following, as will be fully fhown—but before I come to my proofs
I wifh to confute him out of his own writings.

Let

Let me pursue his explanation still further, and afk, what could be the ufe of *fecrefy* in this bufinefs, if Mr. Rumfey, as he alledges, was fecured in the ufe of the invention by law? Could he expect any countenance from the public, for a fcheme wrapped up in fecrefy and which is confeffed by Governor Johnfon to have remained fo until after I had pubiithed *my plan*, both in Maryland and Virginia—Mr. Rumfey and his confidential friends might have died, and then no advantage could have arifen to the community; and until fuch advantage was publicly imparted, certainly nothing could be expected from the public.

In page 16 he inferts part of a letter from general Wafhington in anfwer to his of the 10th. March 1785: " It gives me much pleafure to find by your letter, that you are *not lefs fanguine* in your boat project, than when I faw you at Richmond, and that you have made fuch *further difcoveries* as will render them more extenfively ufeful than was at firft expected"—but ftill it is plain that the General only alluded to the fetting pole plan, for in his anfwer to Governor Johnfon (even after my petition was before the Affembly of Maryland) he *ftill* thought that Mr. Rumfey had " No reliance on Steam"—The General's faying that he thought Mr. Rumfey's idea of fteam was " *Immature*" in November 1784 (the time they were at Richmond,) is a proof that Mr. Rumfey's " *Being not lefs fanguine*" muft have alluded to his *fetting pole* fcheme, becaufe no man can be faid to be *fanguine* in any thing of which he has but " An *immatured* idea;" and " *Further difcoveries*" will not apply to Steam, becaufe *fteam* could be no *new* difcovery, and was mentioned to the General at Richmond: nor is any thing mentioned of Steam in the General's Letter; at leaft in the extract. It is reafonable to fuppofe, if Steam had been the dependable difcovery, it would have been treated on more largely, and have produced a more pointed anfwer; the truth is, Mr. Rumfey placed no dependance on Steam, until my plan came forward, and his own had failed; confcious of the weaknefs of his claim, and the futility of his arguments to fupport it, he found that fomething more was neceffary than merely an " *Immatured idea*;" therefore to add weight to his plea, he endeavours to eftablifh himfelf under the folemnity of oaths, and attempts to prove, that the machinery for his Steam-engine, was executed in Baltimore and Frederick-town, fo as to be compleated and put together on the *1ft. of December* 1785. Thefe folemn and pofitive declarations are contained in the depofitions of Charles Morrow and Jofeph Barns (N°. 11 and 12 of his pamphlet) who are probably interefted in the fcheme. The reader will pleafe to examine thefe depofitions; they are produced to fupport facts, which he is confcious *ought* to have exifted at the time they fpecify, otherwife his pretenfions would confequently fall. Thefe two witneffes teftify to abfolute facts, and yet affix different periods

of

ef time for one and the fame tranfaction. Page 13, line 14, of Charles Morrow's depofition, he fays " About the firft of December (1785) it appears to the faid Charles that the *whole* of the machinery was ready to be fixed to the boat which came down to the falls of Shanandoah for experiment; but the ice then commencing prevented it for the winter:" and line 28 of the fame depofition he fays, " In the fpring of 1786, the machinery was put on the boat and the firft trial made, faid Charles being on board." Page 15, line 11, of *Jofeph Barns's* depofition he fays, " In December (1785) it was *put on the boat* at Shanandoah falls," thefe different declarations, or different times affixed, at which the machinery was *put on the boat*, of themfelves tend much to deftroy the validity of their oaths; for the time the machinery was put on board, muft have been a fact, fo notorious, that it could not admit of a miftake, in a mind properly impreffed with the importance of an oath. In page 10 & 11 William Afkew fwears that Mr. Rumfey's machinery will not weigh more than eight hundred pounds, and that he is well convinced it may be made for £ 20. It is a well know fact that of Mr. Rumfey's machinery, the greateft part, muft confift of copper or brafs, fuch as cylinders, tubes, cocks and valves, together with curious wrought iron; now 800 pounds (were it all made of *Iron*) could not coft lefs than double the fum. As this evidence is not brought to prove any thing about Mr. Rumfey's *priority* it is of no importance, and the abfurdity it contains might have been fpared. Whether *his* machine or *my* machine are beft, is nothing to the purpofe; I have been daily altering, and never watched *his* motions and blunders, as it is evident he did *mine*. He, it feems made a fecret of his doings, whilft mine were open to all the world.

It is proper I fhould not pafs over this part of my work, without acknowledging, that I have been greatly indebted to the affiftance of my ingenious friend Mr. HENRY VOIGHT of this city; who has uniformly, from my firft undertaking to build a boat, afforded me valuable hints; and has united with me in perfecting my plans. To his inventive genius alone, I am indebted for the improvement in our mode of creating fteam; a thought which ftruck him above two years ago, the drawing having been fhewn to feveral perfons; for we *never made a fecret* of any part of our works; but a fear of departing from old eftablifhed plans, made me fearful of adopting it, until I had found by his invention of *creating fteam*, that a *condenfor* might be conftructed on the fame principles, (viz. a fpiral pipe or worm) only by reverfing the agent, for the beft way of applying *fire* to evaporate *water into fteam*, muft alfo be the beft way of applying *cold water* to condenfe *fteam*, that is, the bringing the greateft quantity of fire into action upon the greateft furface of water--or the contrary--And we had an additional inducement to

ftudy

ftudy this fubject, becaufe the common way of fixing boilers, required fo great a load of brick work, that it overloaded our boat. Therefore, the firft thought that muft occur to every man, attempting to raife fteam on board a boat, muft be to acquire that method which would require the leaft weight.—Since Mr. Rumfey has been in town I have been told, that he fays I have got *his mode* of creating fteam; whether that be the cafe or not (or whether he has *got mine)* I do not at prefent know. But as both Mr. Rumfey and Mr. Voight laid their drawings and plans before the Philofophical Society the fame day, it will appear how far they are alike. And Mr. Voight made a prior entry of his plans in the Prothonotary's office, in this city. If there fhould happen to be any fimilarity between them, it would be nothing furprizing; having the fame load on both their minds, they both fought relief; and, as fick perfons, lacking a doctor, chance might have led them to the fame man; and I had an undoubted right to apply every medicine that fuited the diforder—but I will proceed with the pamphlet.—

In Page 17, Henry Bedinger fays, that Mr. James Rumfey informed him in or before the month of March, 1784, that he intended to give trial to a fteam boat, and he believes he mentioned fuch intention of Mr. Rumfey's in Kentuckey; which feems to have been a breach of honour, as it muft be fuppofed Mr. Rumfey gave it to him in confidence; for he treated his idea of Steam as a *fecret* to Governor Johnfon long after: thus on the difclofure of this friend, Mr. Rumfey builds a charge againft me, as having filched his fcheme in Kentuckey; this like his other charges is founded in falfehood, for it is a well known fact, that I have not been in Kentuckey fince the year 1781. The depofitions of George Rootes, N°. 8, and Nicholas Orrick, N°. 10, teftifying to his having informed them, in the year 1784, of his *projecting* a fteam boat is quite ufelefs for reafons already given. Meffrs. Henry and Paine *projected* it before him; and if bare *projection* was fufficient to build a claim on, I have no doubt but there are people now in their graves, whofe heirs might fet up more early claims than either of us. If Mr. Rumfey was in 1784 projecting a boat to work by fteam, with a view of carrying it into actual execution, why did he not apply for the ufe of fteam in his laws? the reafon is plain,—General Wafhington gives it for him, it was " an *immatured idea* and on which he thought he *did not rely.*" I muft therefore contend that thefe depofitions, lofe their weight, and the whole of his conduct proves to a demonftration, that he could not have been engaged in making fteam engines at the time mentioned by thofe witneffes, with a view of applying them to his boat. In page 20, N°. 18, he inferts a paragraph of a letter faid to have been written by a Mr. Daniel Buckley, near Philadelphia, by which he fixes the time of his applying himfelf to the " perfecting his fteam engine with much ardor." In part

of

of faid inferted extract, fpeaking of me, he ftiles me " *a Mr.*
Fitch of Philadelphia;" now this letter, if the facts it recites are
true, muft have been written *after* the 17th. of April, 1786, and
not in 1785, as infinuated by Mr. Rumfey, for I was not an
inhabitant of Philadelphia till after that period; nor did I ever
hear that Mr. Rumfey was employed in making a *fteam boat* until
long after that time; confequently I could not have ufed any ex-
preffions about it until after April, 1786. This is a very important part of the prevarication, and carrying the air of great plaufi-
bility, I muft beg my Reader's clofe attention to it, as I fhall
prove it to be falfe. Page 3, he fays, " I wrote to General
Wafhington the 10th. March, 1785, that I intended applying
both powers (meaning fteam as one) to build a boat after the
model of one he faw at Bath, &c. and as I could gain truth
only by fucceffive experiments, *incredible delays* were produced,
&c. I bore the pelting of ignorance and ill-nature with all re-
fignation, until I was informed fome dark affaffins had endeavoured to wound the reputation of his Excellency, and the other
gentlemen, who faw my exhibition at Bath, for giving me a certificate. The reflections upon thefe worthy gentlemen gave me
inexpreffible uneafinefs, and I fhould certainly have quitted my
fteam engines, *though in great forwardnefs*, and have produced
the beat, for which I had obtained the certificate, for their juftification
and my own, had not a Mr. Fitch came out at *this critical minute,*
with his fteam-boat; afferting that he was the firft inventor of
fteam, and that I had gotten what fmall knowledge I had from
him, &c." Now this embarraffment being confeffedly fubfequent
to the letter to General Wafhington, juft mentioned, viz. 10th.
March, 1785. The letter afferted to have been written by Mr.
Buckley is incontrovertibly fixed between this date and the 1ft. of
December following, the time fworn to for compleating of the
fteam engine; therefore, as Mr. Rumfey quitted his fetting pole
fcheme and " purfued the perfecting his fteam engines with encreafed ardor (page 3) on *the reciept of this letter;* it becomes of
moment to afcertain its exact date; and I fhall fhew that this
letter which fet Meffrs. Rumfey and Barns to work in fuch hafte
and with fuch " encreafed ardor" was not written until near a
year after the time it is pretended, and the copper works faid to
have been made in 1785 were not begun until 1786—fo that this
machinery completed fo brifkly and fworn to have been on board
in December 1785 has made a jump of juft twelve months, in
order to perfuade the public into a belief that Mr. Rumfey's
works were begun time enough to fupplant mine.—" At *that critical minute*" fays he, " Came out a Mr. Fitch afferting I had got
what fmall knowledge I had from him"—At *what* critical minute I afk?—Mr. Rumfey's third page will tell us—In March
1785, he informed General Wafhington by letter that he *intended*
applying fteam to boats; in December following, Meffrs. Barns
and

and Morrow fwear the boat was ready; and his exhibiting this boat, he confeffes was hurried on by the intelligence received from Mr. Buckley; confequently this work and this " Encreafed ardor" was *fubfequent* to the date of the letter from Mr. Buckley. Then if I can fix the time of Mr. Buckley's writing the letter, I fhall eftablifh a certain fixed period at which Mr. Rumfey acknowledges his works were not on board his boat. And I felicitate myfelf in being able to do it fo inconteftibly as to prove from his own writings that he has given *falfe dates* and affigned *falfe reafons* for his movements. He knew at the time of inferting that quibling account, that it would not bear the light, and therefore did not dare to give *the date* of Mr. Buckley's letter, wrote at that " Critical minute," for Mr. Buckley's letter would have fhewn that this " Critical minute" was not in 1785, when they fwear the fteam-boat was ready, but in the Summer of 1786, full twelve months after I had made my plans public, and was procuring patterns for my prefent cylinder, and had made a complete model of a fteam-engine in brafs and iron.— I have been at the pains of walking 66 miles to Pequa and Lancafter to fee Mr. Buckley, that I might obtain an additional proof (to the many others I fhall produce) that Mr. Rumfey has tranfpofed the order of time and antedated facts. Mr. Buckley frankly told me all he knew of the matter and fixed the time of writing his letter, *fo circumftantially*, to have been in 1786 and not in 1785, that not a doubt can remain—and it will further appear from the certificate he has given me that the colouring as to fact, as well as to date, has been grofsly difingenuous, as will be feen on comparing his certificate, No. 18, with the following:

No. 11.

This may certify, that the paragraph that Mr. James Rumfey has copied from my letter, which he applies to the injury of Mr. John Fitch's character, was *not told to me by Mr. Fitch*, but by other perfons, who for reafons were convinced of his priority of invention. And as to the time of writing the letter it was *when Mr. Samuel Briggs was making patterns* for Mr. Fitch's caftings, As witnefs my hand this twelfth day of May, 1788.
DANIEL BUCKLEY.

On my return to Philadelphia I applied to Mr. Briggs in order to afcertain the *Time of his making my patterns*, and he freely gave me the following certificate:

No. 12.

This may certify whom it may concern, That in the *Summer of* 1786, I performed fome turning work for John Fitch, being patterns for caftings for his fteam-boat, and before that time I made no work for the faid John Fitch;—That I am acquainted

C

with Daniel Buckley and faw him at my fhop during that fummer and at fundry times fince, and we have frequently converfed
about James Rumfey, but the particulars of any converfation
with him I do not recollect.

SAMUEL BRIGGS.

Affirmed the 15th. May, 1788, that the foregoing is juft and
true, before

PLUNK T. FLEESON.

Thus, independant of all other proofs, have I brought a con-
clufive evidence out of Mr. Rumfey's own writings and from
his own teftimonies, that the fteam machinery *fworn* to have
been on board *in December*, 1785, could not have been ready until *December*, 1786; and here I might fafely reft my defence,
and very properly quote Mr. Rumfey's own words (annexed to
this certificate, N°· 18.) viz. " Should he incline to *affert* hereafter, what credit he will deferve, has been fo clearly proved,
that *future impofitions* may be avoided, and *thofe* who fpread a
flander they *do not believe*, deferve the contempt of all honeft
men."

But I will proceed, and muft not omit remarking, that
this third page of his work is very fatal to him.   He fays,
" I fhould certainly have quitted my fteam-engines *(engines
only in idea)* though in great forwardnefs, and have produced *the
boat for which I had obtained the certificate, &c.* had not a Mr. Fitch
come out at this critical minute with his fteam-boat, &c." And
further adds, " Had I exhibited my *firft boat* it would have been
conftrued into an acknowledgement of Mr. Fitch's affertion, by
producing a boat with which fteam had nothing to do; thefe
confiderations compelled me to purfue the perfecting my fteam-
engines, with increafed ardor."—Thus I have a proof from
himfelf, that the certificates from General Wafhington, &c.
(which procured his laws in Virginia, Maryland and Pennfylvania) *had no reference to fteam*—confequently *my laws* for the exclufive ufe of fteam applied to boats, cannot interfere either with
his laws, or his expectations at the time of afking for them.   I
applied to the feveral legiflatures openly and unguardedly, without friends and without patrons; and from the pure merit of my
pretenfions, met with fuccefs, without a whifper being breathed,
that I was interfering with Mr. Rumfey.   I am confident that he
never conceived me to be a rival in navigating boats, until he
found his own plan hopelefs and mine likely to fucceed.

In his third page he fays, " I wrote to General Wafhington
10th. March 1785, that I intended applying both powers to a boat
built after the model of the one he faw at Bath; but the difad-
vantages before mentioned ftill remained and as I could gain
truth only by fucceffive experiments, *incredible delays* were produced

ed—and though my diſtreſſes were greatly increaſed thereby,
&c."—It is truly amazing that though he had long before this
letter, been making progreſs in Steam-engines, and gaining
truth by ſucceſſive experiments, and *incredible delays*, inſomuch
that at the time of his propoſing to get cylinders caſt at Governor Johnſon's works in October 1785, he had the principal part
of his work untouched: I ſay it is amazing, that theſe *incredible
delays* ſhould all vaniſh as in an inſtant, and that between the
time of his failing at Governor Johnſon's works, in October or
November 1785, and the 1ſt. of December following, he ſhould
have completed his whole machinery, ready to be put on board.
—A Steam-engine is a complex piece of work, and his ſubſequent tranſactions ſhew that he found it ſo; for it has taken him
from the ſummer of 1786 (when, he removed his works from
Frederick-town) to the winter of 1787 to make them ready for
a fair experiment. No perſon therefore can be brought to believe, that his firſt machinery could have been conjured together
in little more than 30 days.—No ſuch thing happened—I have
already ſufficient proof to the contrary, and have no doubt but
a multitude of corroborating witneſſes will voluntarily offer
themſelves, when this pamphlet gets down to Frederick-town
and Shepherds town, where I ſhall take ſome pains to have it
circulated.—It is truth alone I am in ſearch of, in order to wipe
off the imputations from my own character; for as to ſtability
of title to my excluſive rights, I ſhall not caſt away an anxious
thought about it—I am ſecured by my laws—and my " *coadju-
tors*," as Mr. Rumſey is pleaſed to term them, I am ſure have
no ſort of apprehenſion about the monies they have riſqued; and
only wiſh that I ſhould remove any aſperſions that may be un-
juſtly caſt upon me—Thus far it may be ſaid they have an inter-
eſt in my ſucceſs, becauſe a law in my favour in Maryland is yet
depending.

I muſt not yet quit the ſubject of Mr. Buckley's letter in his
third page, from whence it is plainly to be gathered, that ſubſequent to his letter of 10th. March 1785, to General Waſhington
he meant to tell the world he was buſily employed in *private experiments* on Steam-Engines, and that although his firſt ſetting
pole boat " Bore the pelting of ignorance and ill-nature," yet he
did not ſet about making a Steam-engine, for this boat, until
(as he calls it the *critical moment* when a Mr. Fitch with his Steam-
engine came out, aſſerting that he was the firſt inventor of Steam,
and that " I had gotten what ſmall knowledge I had from him."
—Now as all his experiments were privately conducted, and he
does not pretend to have begun his boat engine, until Mr. Buckley had ſent notice that I charged him with ſtealing knowledge
from me; I would aſk any man where I was to obtain the grounds
for my charge? it could not be until I had begun my own engine,
and made it every where public—then it follows that my pretended

tended complaint againſt him muſt have been ſubſequent to my own works and prior to the beginning of his works for his boat in *November* (as he calls it) which from his own ſtatement has laid a fair and juſt foundation for my claim of public priority, for private priority is out of the queſtion, as Mr. Henry, Mr. Ellicott and Mr. Paine are before us both.

Nay, even after the real Steam-engine for his boat was actually begun, we find it kept as the moſt profound ſecret; and from Charles Morrow's depoſition it is declared, that the boat came to Shepherds-town early in the fall 1785; that Mr. Barns went to Baltimore ſhortly after to have ſome machinery caſt; and on his return from Baltimore was ſent to Frederick-town in order to have ſome other things made (which could not conſiſtently with Governor Johnſon's letter be earlier than the beginning of November) and about the middle of November they were all finiſhed viz. *a boiler, two cylinders, pumps, pipes, &c.*—I confeſs this is very briſk work for a country town—more than ever I could get in the city of Philadelphia.

At Baltimore four large cocks were beſpoke by Mr. Barns and the braſs-founder was told they were for the *warm ſprings of Virginia* as will preſently appear; Governor Johnſon was entruſted with the ſcheme in confidence, and the copper works were carried on in Frederick-town with great ſecreſy—inſomuch that a citizen hearing it rumored that they were for a Steam-engine, applied to ſee them, but was refuſed (as will be ſhewn) and the matter ſtill remained a ſecret until, as Governor Johnſon ſays; "The deſigned purpoſe of the cylinder was a ſubject of pretty general converſation in Frederick-town"—Then during this interval of privacy, ſurely any man that ſhould have conceived the ſame idea and brought it forward to public view, ought to be entitled to the right and advantages of the diſcovery—For all theſe confidential perſons, as I have already ſaid, might have died, and the world have loſt the benefit—Let me conſider the danger of admitting this new doctrine of claims—A man makes a valuable diſcovery—he purſues it at a great expence and publiſhes it to the world—a ſett of men combining together ſhall afterwards come forth, ſwear for each other, that they had been making the ſame kind of engine, many months before, and bring proofs from reſpectable characters, that they had *hinted* at the practicability of ſuch a ſcheme, even before their private experiments. Will any man of the leaſt particle of underſtanding allow, that this *private work* ſhall be admitted to contain ſufficient evidence to overſet the public works of a fair and open artiſt? Surely not —If it was once allowed, men would not be wanting to ſwear away from the real inventor, the moſt valuable diſcoveries in the world.—All they would deſire from the public claimant, would be, for him to fix the earlieſt date to his diſcovery, and if it was 20 or even 50 years back they would prove that they themſelves,

their

their fathers or grandfathers, or some distant friend, had communicated it many years before.—There is no end to this kind
of proof; and both reason and law unite in defending the first
public discoverer.—It would be dangerous in the highest degree
to deviate from this rule.—If Mr. Rumsey did really in good
faith and conscience intend to carry into execution, the secret he
communicated to General Washington, I can only say he was
unlucky in delaying it so long, as to let me, with my subsequent
discoveries, come forward before him; what I did was public—it
was notorious to all Virginia and Maryland, and not a murmur
was raised against me, not a syllable uttered (that I ever heard)
charging me with interfering with Mr. Rumsey.—The Assem-
blies of Virginia and Maryland encouraged my scheme, and nobody told me I should interfere with him.—My petitions laid
long before the Assembly of Virginia, and a law was ultimately
passed in my favour, without objection or complaint. Mr. Rumsey has insinuated that I got my first thought from Captain Bedinger in Kentuckey, who went there in 1784—nay he goes so
far *in one place*, as to say, he " Was told so" and in *another* that
" Circumstances leave little room to doubt it." I have already
declared that I have not been in Kentuckey since the year 1781:
thus falls to the ground, this part of his " Plagiarism" allega-
tions.—But I will suggest to him, that it is much more probable, that all *his* determinations of beginning his Steam-engine,
might have come *to him* in a much straighter line, than from
Kentuckey to me. Captain Bedinger is so uncertain about the
matter of his ever having mentioned *steam* in Kentuckey, that he
only says, coldly, that he " *believes*" he also mentioned " that
it *worked by steam.*" I will remind Mr. Rumsey, that I not only
believe that I presented my plan to Congress, *before* the time he
pretends to have spoken to Governor Johnson about getting cylinders for him, and *before* his copper works were bespoke, but
the Files of Congress will *prove*, that in August, 1785, I
laid my plan before them; and nobody will suppose it was a very
indirect road from Congress to each of the United States. A
very few days after my plan was laid before them, Mr. Rumsey
might have been furnished with a copy of it: and if any member of Congress should know of such a transaction (certainly
very innocent in itself) he will confer a great obligation on me by
communicating it.—But in Philadelphia it was public before it
went to Congress, and long before Mr. Rumsey's orders went to
Frederick Town or Baltimore. I have a fair right to suppose all
these things, and Mr. Rumsey's giving me no opposition in my
application for exclusive laws, and even permitting his law to
expire in Pennsylvania, without trying to derive any benefit
from it, amount to positive proof that he had no serious thoughts
about applying steam until it was too late.—I promise him I shall
not be so dilatory in exhibiting *my boats* in Virginia, conform-
ably

ably to my law. I truft to the goodnefs of my caufe and the honor and generofity of my country,—and that I not only have a fubftantial right by exclufive laws, but by juftice and equity.

The affidavits from William Afkew, N°. 6, and Henry Bedinger, N°. 7, to prove that Mr. Rumfey's boat is much fuperior to mine, is acknowledging on the part of Mr. Rumfey, that his pretenfions to the invention are but weakly founded. However faulty my works might be, and however perfect his own, it would have no force in the determination of our title to the invention; but argues a wifh in him to gain an advantage on principles different from thofe on which our difpute muft be ultimately *decided* in the *opinion* of the world.—But even this pofition of Mr. Rumfey's I will not allow: for on a comparifon of the velocity, and bulk of both boats and the force applied, it is evident that mine exceeded in the proportion of more than two to one. I had a bulk of water to remove equal to above 12 tons, whilft he had to contend with no more than 3 tons, if I am rightly informed; and our cylinders (or moving powers) were nearly, if not quite, equal: yet my boat was urged forward with nearly the fame velocity of his boat;—therefore, his mode hath hitherto no fuperiority. As to his drawing water in at the bottom, and puthing it out at the ftern of a veffel, it is no new invention, but was long before prefented to the Philofophical Society at Philadelphia. The thought came originally from France, of which I was acquainted before he befpoke any of his works for fteam, and contended the right of ufing it with Mr. Arthur Donaldfon, in the beginning of 1786, before the Affembly of Pennfylvania, as he attempted, at that time, to affume the difcovery to himfelf.

N°. 13.

I well remember when Mr. Arthur Donaldfon propofed before the committee of Affembly, a method of navigating boats by a ftream of water forced through by means of a fteam engine; that you appeared to be acquainted with the principle, which was faid to be originally Dr. Franklin's, and that you then declared it had been your intention to have made an experiment upon it.

GEO. CLYMER.

Mr. John Fitch.
May 17, 1788.

In fpite of all oppofition I was left in full poffeffion of that or any other way I chofe, provided I worked by fteam, and no man can take it from me until my laws expire. I conceive we have by no means come to the greateft perfection of applying our power. I am now trying an experiment, and the machine is nearly finifhed, to propel a boat not by expelling *water*, but *air*, and hope Mr. Rumfey will allow that this is a mode peculiar to
myfelf;

myfelf; but if he pleafes he will deny it and affert that he had privately tried fome experiments to affertain its practicability—I further hope that the public will make great allowances for my not being more forward in my plans, efpecially when they confider the great difficulty of procuring proper workmen, together with the new and unexplored ground that I had to travel over, but hope fhortly that I fhall have it fo perfect as to give full fatisfaction of its utility.

In Page 5, he afferts, that my boat will not be propelled at the rate of more than three miles per hour when no tide oppofes: this affertion, I believe, will fhortly be proved both rafh and envious: I can make her go not only three, but three times three.

But as I have before mentioned, this is taking up the difpute upon different principles, than thofe Mr. Rumfey found neceffary to hold up to public view, viz. That he was the inventor of the fteam-boat.—This leads me to confider the principles on which exclufive privileges are founded, agreeably to juftice and policy. If we have recourfe to the enlightened nations of Europe, and more efpecially to England, whofe laws refpecting the title to property are (with little and in fome cafes with no variation) in force among us, we fhall find that their laws imply that no fpecies of property ought to be held more facred than the property of inventions: for having their origin in the imagination of man, uncertain in their operations, and expenfively perplexing in experiment, it becomes neceffary to have fome mode eftablifhed to fecure to the owner the full benefit of his invention, which might otherwife prove his ruin. To prevent which, juftice and good policy have pointed out a remedy, and cuftom has eftablifhed it on a permanent bafis.—The inventor can claim no benefit from his thoughts or inventions, before he makes a public declaration of fuch invention in fome place of record eftablifhed for fuch purpofes,—that is—he who invented and publifhed a *Steam-Engine* will have an exclufive right for a certain number of years for all fteam-engines: at the *expiration* of which, each *improver* has an undoubted right to the benefit of any *improvement*. On thefe principles he who firft invented and publifhed the idea of a fteam-boat, invefts himfelf with a fair and juft title to all fteam-boats for a certain time, which in juftice and policy government is bound to fupport.—The ftate of Pennfylvania hath given her fentiments on this head, and hath declared fuch to have been her explanation of the title to inventions by rejecting Mr. Arthur Donaldfon's petition to have me confined to a certain mode of applying my power.—It was not the mode of *ufing the force of fteam* which had any merit in this invention; but, it was the idea of connecting *fteam* with *navigation*, that juftly claimed the public patronage as foon as that idea was made public, and the benefit of it applied for.

I fhall

I shall now introduce the proofs I have promised, and show to the world what degree of credit and countenance ought to be given to a man, who in order to deprive me of my just rights, has brought forward evidences to swear to facts which are totally false—You will see that transactions are antedated and a deception intended, with a view both of disgracing and robbing me— Confident that gross misrepresentations had been made use of, I was at the expence and trouble of two journeys to Frederick-town in Maryland, the scene of his operations, and there I was soon confirmed in my suspicions that this plausible pamphlet was built on falshood, and, that the patrons whom Mr. Rumsey's address has procured him in this city, have committed themselves too unreservedly to a stranger. I now find the reason of his so long delaying to put in his claim—it was that a period might elapse sufficient for memory to be uncertain, and for facts to be transposed in the order of time; the death of one of his principal workmen also rendered it probable that some of his pretended proofs might be difficult to detect. A love of justice has induced a number of persons to step forward and testify in the most unequivocal manner that the works sworn by Mr. Rumsey's evidences to have been finished the 1st. December, 1785, were not begun until March following, when he must have been very fully possessed of a knowledge of my pretensions.

The ten following certificates will prove fully the antedating.

No. 14.

The affidavit of Frederick Tombough, Smith and partner of Mr. Zimmer, the Copper-smith in Frederick Town who made the copper work for Mr. Rumsey's steam-boat.

Maryland, Frederick County, April 18th. 1788. Then appeared before the subscriber, a justice for said state and county, Frederick Tombough, aged about thirty-nine years, who being sworn on the holy Evangelists of Almighty God, deposeth and sayeth, that some time in March 1786, he, this deponent was in partnership with Matthias Zimmers, now deceased, in a black-smith's shop, adjoining said Zimmers' copper-smith's shop—and that he remembers two copper pipes being brought into his shop by said Zimmers to fix the seams—which pipes he was told were for Mr. Rumsey's Steam boat—and further that he knew of no work being done in Mr. Zimmers' shop on account of said boat previous to the time above mentioned.

Sworn before

GEORGE SCOTT.

No. 15.

The certificate of Mrs. Zimmers, widow of Mr. Zimmers, which is corroborated, and the time established, by the next certificate:

This

(25)

This may certify, that I the fubfcriber, wife to the late Matthias Zimmers, deceafed, have no accounts in my books fo as to affertain the time of Mr. Rumfey's befpeaking his machinery for his Steam-boat, or as to the time of his taking it away—but that Michael Baltzel turned works to finifh the firft machinery faid Rumfey had of my hufband according to the beft of my knowledge.—As witnefs my hand, this 29th. April, 1788.

ELIZABETH ZIMMERS.

N°· 16.

The certificate of Michael Baltzel, Turner, which eftablifhes the time of Mrs. Zimmers' fact.

Frederick-town, 17th. *April*, 1788.

This may certify that I the fubfcriber turned works for Mr. James Rumfey of Virginia, for his Steam-boat viz. a round piece of wood about 8 inches diameter and about 4 feet long, &c. to round his copper works upon—faid turning was done in March 1786. As witnefs my hand

MICHAEL BALTZEL.

N°· 17.

The certificate of Mr. Jonathan Morris, inn-keeper, which confirms the affertion in Governor Johnfon's letter, that the " Defigned purpofe of the cylinders was a fubject of pretty general converfation" in Frederick Town, and therefore had it been prior to my petition to the affembly of Maryland the middle of December, 1785, Mr. Foy, the member of affembly refident in that town muft have known it, and the houfe have received information from him, when probably they might have affigned other reafons for rejecting my petition than mere barenefs of finances. If all the machinery was ready to put on board, as Mr. Morrow fwears, on the 1ft. December, it muft have been a fact notorious to the whole town;—but the following declaration fhows that fo far from being on board in December, 1785, it was fhut up as a fecret even fo late as the latter end of March following; fo that this " pretty general converfation," which Governor Johnfon fpeaks of, could not have happened until about this time, and all the evidences I produce confirm my affertion, that Mr. Rumfey did not begin his fteam-engine, until I had publifhed my plan all through Maryland and Virginia.—The certificate is as follows:

Frederick-town 18th. *April* 1788.

This may certify that I the fubfcriber was towards the latter end of March 1786, informed that Mr. Matthias Zimmers had

D   begun

begun fome machinery for Mr. Rumfey's Steam boat—Accordingly I called on Mr. Zimmers to fee it, but was refufed the fight
of it, as it was then retained as Mr. Rumfey's fecret—but was
informed that it was begun in the beginning of the fame month,
this I declare to be the truth as near as I can recollect—As witnefs my hand

JONATHAN MORRIS.

Nᵒ· 18.

The depofition of John Peters, who performed fuch parts of
Mr. Rumfey's machinery as were made of tin.

Frederick County, Maryland, April 18th. 1788.
I the fubfcriber was a journeyman and worked for Mr Matthias Zimmers—and began to work, in the tin bufinefs, at the
fame time Mr. Zimmers did begin the copper works for Mr.
James Rumfey, of Virginia, for his Steam boat, which faid
coppers and tin works weie begun in March, in the year 1786.

JOHN PETERS.

Sworn before me, JACOB YOUNG, one of the juftices
for Frederick county, Maryland.

Nᵒ· 19.

The depofition of John Frymiller, who was apprentice to Mr.
Zimmers at the time he made the copper works for the fteam-
engine, fhewing not only that the works were begun and finifhed
in a fhop next to Mr. Tombough; but that no part of faid machinery was begun *before* the fpring, 1786.

State of Maryland, Baltimore County.
On this twenty-fixth day of April, in the year of our Lord one
thoufand feven hundred and eighty eight, before me the fubfcriber
one of the juftices of the peace for the county aforefaid, perfonally appeared John Frymiller of Baltimore town in faid county,
and made oath on the holy Evangelifts of Almighty God, that
during the time he was an apprentice to the late Mr. Matthias
Zimmers of Frederick-town, in Frederick county and ftate aforefaid, deceafed, when he the faid Matthias Zimmer made Mr.
James Rumfey's machinery for the Steam-boat—That he, this
deponent, did work at the faid James Rumfey's machinery—That
it was begun in the fpring of the year 1786, and that no part of
faid machinery was begun before the time above-mentioned by
the faid Zimmers, to the beft of his knowledge—and further, that
the faid machinery was begun and finifhed in a fhop adjoining
Frederick Tombough's fmith-fhop, (which faid Tombough was,
as the deponent has been informed, in partnerfhip in the fmith's
businefs

bufinefs at faid time with faid Zimmers) in which faid Matthias Zimmers had his copper-fmith's fires for brazing &c. and further this deponent faith not.

Sworn before me

JOHN MOALE.

The following certificate proves that Mr. Rumfey's machinery was made by Mr. Zimmers, in Frederick Town, in the fpring of 1786, their being but two Copper-fmiths in Frederick Town, viz. Meffrs. Matthias Zimmers and Jofhua Minfhall, the certifier.

Nᵒ. 20.

This may certify, that I the fubfcriber, copper-fmith, have refided in this town about three years, during which time there has no copper-fmiths refided in the town except Mr. Matthias Zimmers and myfelf and that I was knowing to Mr. Zimmers making copper works for Mr. Rumfey's Steam boat, and am of opinion it was late in the fpring or fummer before faid Rumfey took faid works from Mr. Zimmers in the year 1786. As witnefs my hand, 29th. April 1788, at Frederick-town, Maryland.

JOSHUA MINSHALL.

The foregoing teftimonies, I prefume, will carry full conviction that Mr. Rumfey has fhifted his dates, and has got two of his workmen to fwear to it—for Meffrs. Barns and Morrow, if they had confulted their accounts, muft have found that they had made a lapfe of a whole year at leaft, and that the December, 1785, which they fpeak of muft have been December, 1786. —The circumftance of being ftopped by the ice proves it to have been in the winter, and therefore muft inevitably have been in the winter of 1786. But this was too late a date to ferve their purpofe of fupplanting my claims and juft rights, which I mean to maintain under the laws I have already obtained and have no doubt of fucceeding in my applications to the other affemblies when they come to fee my proofs and Mr. Rumfey's falfe datings. He has mentioned the obtaining part of his works from Baltimore, where I can alfo fhew he has ufed the fame want of candor, and it will confirm the proofs from Frederick Town.

It appears the four large cocks for his fteam-pipes and works, were befpoke of Chriftopher Raborg, in Baltimore, by Mr. Barns, who, the better to conceal the " defigned purpofe of the cylinders," told him they were for the warm fprings in Virginia, —perhaps a little mental refervation might cover this deviation from fact.—But Mr. Raborg had no account thereof and could not give the time with precifion—though he believes they were made in the fall of 1785;—the cerificates, Nᵒ. 20 and 21, which follow, prove that the time was certainly in the fpring 1786. As thefe certificates appear to refer only to cocks made for the warm

fprings,

springs, I had confiderable doubts about admitting them into my
defence; becaufe Mr. Rumfey, on finding that I proved them to
be made in March, 1786, might (if he pleafed) adhere to Mr.
Barns's declaration of their being made for the warm fprings
and not for the fteam-boat: But I am now happy in having a
confirmation under Mr. Rumfey's own hand, publifhed in Mr.
Ofwald's pap r of the tenth inftant, where he informs the public,
" Mr. Raborg was the perfon who undertook to make cocks for
my fteam boat, and by him I fhall prove that they were finifhed
at the time he mentioned to Mr. Fitch, viz. the fall of 1785."
    Chriftopher Raborg's certificate is as follows:

N°. 21.

This may certify, that Mr. Jofeph Barns did befpeak of me
four brafs cocks, which he faid were for the warm fprings;—
that being difappointed by my journeymen, I got them made by
Mr. Charles Weir & Co.—faid cocks I do believe were made in
the fall 1785, but have no charge made of them to affertain the
time with precifion--this I affert, as witnefs my hand, at Baltimore,
this 26th. day of April 1788.

CHRIST. RABORG.

N°. 22.

The certificate of Charles Wier, who fpeaks with tolerable
certainty of the works being made in the fpring of 1786.

This may certify, that when I was in partnerfhip with Ifaac
Cauften, I made four brafs cocks for Mr. Chriftopher Raborg,
for which I received the money and charged myfelf with it—
that my books are deftroyed and I cannot exactly recollect the
time of their being made, but am perfuaded it was early in the
fpring in the year 1786—this further may certify, that I never
made the exact number of four cocks for faid Raborg, except
only that one time. As witnefs my hand, at Baltimore, 26th. day
of April 1788.

CHARLES WEIR.

N°. 23.

The certificate of Ifaac Cauften, who afcertains upon good
grounds that the faid work was done and charged on the 29th.
March, 1786.

This may certify, that I the fubfcriber with my partner Charles
Weir, made four brafs cocks for Mr. Chriftopher Raborg, and
charged them on the partnerfhip account—faid book has fince
been deftroyed, but from fome loofe papers I found charged to
Mr. Raborg on the Company's account, on the 29th. March
1786, four brafs cocks, which with other accounts I have drawn
out

out into my day book. Neither have I made the exact number of four cocks for him at any other time. In witnefs whereof I have hereunto fet my hand this 26th. day of April 1788.

ISAAC CAUSTEN.

The reader will doubtlefs, on an examination of the two pamphlets, perceive things in their true light, and that Mr. Rumfey made no pretence to ufe fteam till after the failure of his boat on the principles exhibited at Bath, after I had invefted my-felf with an undoubted title, by exhibiting the invention to Congrefs in Auguft, 1785, and had publifhed it to the ftates of Virginia and Maryland, who became virtually bound to fecure me the right. Mr. Rumfey profecuting his works in fecret, and appearing at this late day, with antedated facts, is a full proof that he had no claim to the invention, nor is there any one principle of law or equity, on which he can found his pretenfions. If he claims it on his *thought* Mr. Paine, Mr. Henry and Mr. Andrew Ellicott are long before him;—if on forming drafts without communicating them to the public, he muft acknowledge Mr. Henry's priority: but if it is to be decided, as it certainly muft, by the eftablifhed mode of public declaration on record, my title is indifputable. Being, therefore, certain of the ftability of my claim, founded on the modes eftablifhed in juftice and policy, I have not a doubt but my country will fecure and protect the right fhe has fo deliberately granted to me. Under this fecurity I embarked my time, my fortune and reputation, and thus embarked, I am certain I have nothing to fear; but fhall depend with full confidence on a continuance of that juftice which is due to the rights of the citizen, and the honor of my country.

JOHN FITCH.

Philadelphia, 10th. *May,* 1788.

POSPSCRIPT.

P O S T S C R I P T.

SINCE this Pamphlet went to prefs a fecond edition of Mr.
Rumfey's pamphlet has been printed in this city, in which
a fhort advertifement is prefixed and an extract of his own letter
to General Wafhington which are as follow:

A D V E R T I S E M E N T.

THE following pages are taken from a pamphlet publifhed in
Virginia, to prove the author's prior right of applying fteam, to
propel boats, &c. as well as to eftablifh the principles on which
he has done it, a few copies were then thought fufficient for that
purpofe, but as Mr. Fitch intends to anfwer the pamphlet, it is
therefore neceffary to re-publifh as much of it as refpects Mr.
Fitch, which is done with no other variation, from the original,
than to correct a few of the omiffions and miftakes that were
introduced into the firft publication, from the hurry in which it
was done, (as the author at that time could not attend the prefs)
and was circulated with an apology annexed to the poftcript, for
the imperfection of the impreffion; of thefe corrections, perhaps
Mr. Fitch may take fome notice, if he fhould, fuch part of the
old pamphlet fhall be reprinted (verbatim) to convince the Public that the fubject has not been varied; but a little better explained. The fophiftry in Mr. Fitch's reply (fhould it contain
what he informs me it does) is evidently calculated to make im-
preffions, unfavourable of me, on the Public mind, and to
wound the reputation of feveral refpectable characters, I muft
therefore beg the Public's indulgence, to fufpend their opinion
for a few weeks, when I fhall have it in my power to lay before
them fuch additional ftatement of facts, fupported by fuch refpectable teftimony, as will inconteftible prove the unjuftifiable fteps
Mr. Fitch has taken, to deprive the author of his difcoveries,
and to injure the reputation of fundry gentlemen.

N°. 19. is added to this publication; it is part of a letter wrote
by the editor to his excellency General Wafhington, dated the
tenth of March 1785, which will fhew that the editor had fixed
on a method of applying fteam to propel a boat before Mr. Fitch
knew (from his own account of the matter) that fteam had ever
been made ufe of for any purpofe whatever; how then is it poffi-
ble he fhould have the prior right to this difcovery? if it is afked,
who made the moft promifing experiment? it would be found
that my experiments two years fince exceed the beft he has ever

made;

made; muſt I then be deprived of my diſcoveries, which are ſubſtantial, becauſe I endeavoured to keep them ſecret until per-fected? juſtice will never ſuffer it, I therefore with the greateſt confidence look up to my countrymen for their ſupport, accor-ding to the merits of my cauſe, and have the honor of ſubſcrib-ing myſelf their

moſt devoted humble ſervant

J A M E S   R U M S E Y.

Philadelphia, May 7, 1788.

As to his advertiſement I have fully proved that he made no experiment on his boat with Steam two years ago, his machine-ry being at that time in Frederick-town—And his boat ſo far exceeding mine will alſo appear a wrong aſſertion as the greateſt diſtance he pretends to have propelled his ſmall boat per hour is four miles, and that appears to be mere ideal eſtimation. In my boat, by the ſame force applied, I let out three miles and a quarter per hour by the log-line. This is departing from the merits of the diſpute, but to convince the public of his aſſerti-on on this head being abſurd, I ſhall introduce certificates Nᵒ· 24, 25, 26. As to his requeſt of ſuſpending the public opinion, I reſt my cauſe on ſolid and fair concluſions drawn from his pamphlet, a very ſafe and candid judgment may be formed of the merits of Mr. Rumſey's pretentions, it being evident that all his falſe aſſertions and falſe dating will never prove that two and two are not four.

Nᵒ· 24.

Theſe may certify, that the ſubſcriber has frequently ſeen Mr. Fitch's Steam boat, which with great labour and perſeverance he has at length compleated and has likewiſe been on board when the boat was worked againſt both wind and tide, with a very conſiderable degree of velocity by the force of Steam only, Mr. Fitch's merit in conſtructing a good Steam-engine and ap-plying it to ſo uſeful a purpoſe will no doubt meet with the en-couragement he ſo juſtly deſerves from the generoſity of his countrymen, eſpecially thoſe who wiſh to promote every improve-ment of the uſeful arts in America.

D A V I D   R I T T E N H O U S E.

Philadelphia, December 12th. 1787.

Nᵒ· 25.

Having alſo ſeen the boat urged by the force of Steam and having been on board of it when in motion, I concur in the above opinion of Mr. Fitch's merits.

J O H N   E W I N G.

From

No. 26.

From the well known force of Steam. I was one of the firſt of thoſe who encouraged Mr. Fitch to reduce his theory of a Steam-boat to practiſe, in which he has ſucceeded far beyond my expectations. I am now fully of opinion that Steam-boats may be made to anſwer valuable purpoſes in facilitating the internal navigation of the United States, and that Mr. Fitch has great merit in applying a Steam engine to ſo valuable a purpoſe and entitled to every encouragement from his country and countrymen.

ANDREW ELLICOTT.

Philadelphia, December 13*th.* 1787.

Copy of Mr. Rumſey's Extract, N°. 19.

The following is part of a letter, wrote by the editor, to his Excellency General Waſhington, dated the 10th. of March, 1785.

After mentioning that kind of machine for propelling boats which the General had ſeen a model of, I proceed to ſay—" I have taken the greateſt pains to perfect another kind of boat, *upon the principles I mentioned to you at Richmond* in November laſt, and have the pleaſure to inform you that I have brought it to great perfection; it is true, it will coſt ſomething more than the other way, but, when in uſe, will be more manageable, and can be worked with as few hands; the power is immenſe—and I have quite convinced myſelf that boats of paſſage may be made to go againſt the current of the *Miſſiſſippi* or *Ohio* rivers, or in the *Gulf Stream* (from the *Leeward* to the *Windward-Iſlands*) from ſixty to one hundred miles per day. I know this will appear ſtrange and improbable to many perſons, yet I am very certain it may be performed, beſides, it is ſimple (when underſtood) and is alſo ſtrictly Philoſophical.

The principles of this boat I am very cautious not to explain, as it would be eaſily executed by an ingenious perſon.

The plan I mean to purſue, is to put both the machines on board of boats * built on a large ſcale, and then, Sir, if you would be kind enough to ſee them make actual performances, I ſhould not doubt but the aſſemblies would allow me ſomething handſome, which would be more advantageous to the public than to give me the excluſive right of uſing them.

As

---

* There were two boats connected, in the model I exhibited at Bath in September 1787, which is the reaſon I ſpeak of boats in the plural, as experiment had convinced me that a ſingle boat would not ſucceed on that principle.

As to the extract of his letter to General Washington of the tenth of March, 1785, it is nothing more than a declaration that he intended something;—that even if it was steam he meant to make use of, it was a profound secret which he was then cautious not to explain. But let us take a view of this letter and I have no doubt, but from the very wording of it, it will very clearly appear, that the utility of steam (if that was what he meant to convey) was with him at that time very doubtful and upon which he could have no kind of dependance; and holding up the idea of secrecy so punctually, least some artist, more ingenious than himself, should compleat a steam-boat before him, shews indubitably that he conceived it as an agent at a great distance from him and upon which he had no reliance or from which the public could then expect no advantage, and indeed I am confident that his ideas of a steam engine, (if any he had, which I much doubt) were very inferior to Messrs. Henry's, Ellicott's, Pain's, &c. in the year 1778. but as no publication to the world took place by them, they are candid enough not to claim it as an invention of theirs. But should I even go so far as to admit he had thoughts of applying steam, and that he intended exhibiting a steam-boat to General Washington, it was nothing more than an intention he held in secret, on the 10th. of March, 1785, and even by his declarations to Governor Johnson, if they were. as early as October or November, 1785, he kept it then a secret —nothing was imparted to the Public, therefore nothing due from them. I had long before declared my intentions through Congress, and thereby invested myself with the indisputable title to my invention throughout the United States. Maryland and Virginia had virtually pledged the honor of their states to secure me in this right.—Virginia has since supported that honor, by cheerfully passing a law for that purpose, and Maryland, I doubt not, as also other of the United States, will pay equal regard to justice and policy.

N. B. As the application of steam to vessels will undoubtedly claim the early attention of the world, as the least expensive and safest mode of navigation,—I doubt not but the impartial public will yet, with pleasure, secure in me those rights, for which security, had I applied on the first exhibition of my scheme, would have been granted without murmur or delay; but as a confidence in the honor of my country, and a want of finance, were then the preventatives, the delay certainly will not operate now against me; as the utility of the invention more clearly appears, and thereby the attention of my country more reasonably claimed.

E

The

The following certificates were omitted in their proper places.

N°. 1.

I do certify, that as I was returning with John Fitch from Neſhamany meeting ſome time in April, 1785, as near as I can recollect the time, when a gentleman and his wife paſſed by us in a riding chair; he immediately grew inattentive to what I ſaid. Some time after he informed me that at that inſtant the firſt idea of a ſteam-boat ſtruck his mind.

JAMES OGILBEE.

N°. 2.

An Extract of a Letter from James Scout.

You are deſirous of knowing from me when the firſt thought of a Steam-boat came in your head; this I cannot tell, but this you told me, that in the month of April, 1785, you was travelling down Street road in company with Mr. James Ogilbee and Mr. Sinton paſſing you on Street road, that then the firſt thought occurred to you of a Steam-boat, and the month of May or June following you ſhewed me a plan of your machine on paper, this truth I ſhall ſeek no further teſtimony to ſupport; 'tis too generally known; let them that doubt it come and hear more from

Your humble Servant,

JAMES SCOUT.

April 15th. 1788.

N°. 5.

This is to certify, that Mr. John Fitch called upon William Henry, Eſquire, my late huſband in his life time, about two years and an half ſince, when Mr. Fitch ſhewed to him drafts and a model of a machine how to propel a boat through the water: And further, that I have frequently heard Mr. Henry applying ſteam, as a mean to urge boats through the water by force of it, and that he had propoſed laying a model of a machine, for that purpoſe, before the Philoſophical Society long before Mr. Fitch called upon him.

Witneſs my hand, this 12th Day of May, 1788.

Teſt.
ANN HENRY.
JNO. JOS. HENRY.

F I N I S.

A

PLAN

WHEREIN THE POWER OF

STEAM

IS FULLY SHEWN,

By a new conftructed Machine, for propelling Boats or Veffels, of any burthen, againft the moft rapid ftreams or rivers, with great velocity. Alfo, a Machine, conftructed on fimilar philofophical principles, by which water may be raifed for Grift or Saw-Mills, watering of Meadows, &c. &c.

BY JAMES RUMSEY,

OF BERKELEY COUNTY, VIRGINIA.

TO THE PUBLIC.

THOSE who have had the good fortune to difcover a new machine, or to make any material improvements on fuch as have been already difcovered, muft lay their account to encounter innumerable difficulties; they muft arm themfelves with patience to abide difappointments; to correct a thoufand imperfections (which the trying hand of experience alone can point out) to endure the fmarting fhafts of wit, and, what is perhaps more intolerable than all the reft put together (on the leaft failure of any experiments) to bear up againft the heavy abufe and bitter fcoffs of ill-natured ignorance. Thefe never fail to reprefent the undertaker as an impofter, and his motives the moft knavifh: Happy for him if he efcape with fo gentle an appellative as that of a madman.

This is the fate of the unlucky projector, even in the cities of Europe, where every material is at his command, and every artificer at his fervice. A candid public will then confider my

A

tuation;

fituation; thrown by hard fate beyond the mountains, and deprived of every advantage which that grand mover, water, produces, they will eafily conceive how my difficulties have been multiplied, which is the only reafon of my not exhibiting my long promifed BOAT before this; and which I hope, will be a fufficient apology. Even now, thefe difficulties render my machinery very incomplete; but Mr. Fitch's endeavouring to procure patents for his boat, (of which I fhall fpeak hereafter) and having actually procured an exclufive right from two refpectable Affemblies, (who had granted me the fame in the year 1784.) Before I was aware what he was about, I was neceffitated to exhibit, circumftanced as I was; and my machine, with all its misfortunes upon its head, is abundantly fufficient to prove my pofition; which was. " That a boat might be fo conftructed, as to be propelled through the water at the rate of ten miles in an hour, by the force of *fteam*; and that the machinery employed for that purpofe, might be fo fimple and cheap, as to reduce the price of freightage, at leaft, one half in common navigation; likewife, that it might be forced, by the fame machinery, with confiderable velocity, againft the conftant ftreams of long and rapid rivers.

Such a machine I propofed to prepare, and fuch a boat to exhibit; this I have now fo far performed, in the prefence of fo many witneffes, and to the fatisfaction of fo many difinterefted gentlemen, as to convince the unprejudiced, and deprive even the fceptic of his doubt.

If the reader will be pleafed to turn to the annexed certificates, No. 1, 2; 3, he will be convinced that on Monday, the 3d. day of December laft, my boat was propelled with near half her burthen on board, againft the current of Potowmack river, at the rate of three miles in an hour, notwithftanding the bad order the machinery was then in; and by the certificates, No. 4, and 5, on the eleventh of the fame month, by what little repairs I could give it, in a country where conveniences were not to be had, her progrefs againft the fame ftream was encreafed to four miles in an hour, with more than half her burthen on board. What additions may not be expected, if I am enabled, by the generofity of the different Affemblies to perfect my plan?

In the month of September, 1784, I exhibited the model of a boat before his Excellency General Wafhington, at Bath, in Berkeley county, calculated for ftemming the currents of rapid rivers only, conftructed on principles very different from my prefent one. Satisfied with the experiment of her making way againft a rapid ftream, by the force of the faid fteam, the General was pleafed to give me a moft ample certificate of her efficacy; and though the great utility of fuch a boat will appear, if ever a fair trial fhould be made of it: and though at the time of my exhibition it was fully my intention to complete this boat,

yet,

yet, in the course of that fall and winter, I made such progress in some steam engines, which I had long before conceived would become of the greatest consequence, that I postponed it, till experiments should determine whether the steam engines could be reduced to such simplicity and cheapness, as to make them of public benefit; not being certain of this, though perfectly convinced of the power, was my only reason for not mentioning this scheme also to the General, at that exhibition; and I flattered myself this invention, if it answered my expectations, (the truth whereof experiments have now established) would render my labours more extensively useful, by being equally applicable to small boats or vessels of the largest size, to shallow and rapid rivers or the deepest and roughest seas, (indeed, in large vessels, compared with the value of the freightage, the expence of the machinery proportionally decreases) I applied myself with unremitted attention to perfect my steam vessels, and made such progress in that fall and the ensuing spring, that my experiments assured me the perfection of such a machine was within my reach. I therefore wrote to General Washington, the 10th of March 1785, that I intended applying both powers to a boat built after the model of the one he saw at Bath; but as the disadvantages before mentioned still remained, and as I could gain truth only by successive experiments, incredible delays were produced; and though my distresses were greatly encreased thereby, I bore the pelting of ignorance and ill-nature with all resignation, until I was informed some dark assassins had indeavoured to wound the reputation of his Excellency, and the other gentlemen who saw my exhibition at Bath, for giving me a certificate. The reflections upon those worthy gentlemen gave me inexpressible uneasiness, and I should certainly have quitted my steam-engines, though in great forwardness, and have produced the boat for which I had obtained the certificate, for their justification and my own, had not a Mr. Fitch came out at this critical minute with his steam-boat, asserting, that "he was the first inventor of steam, and that I had gotten *what small knowledge I had* from him, but that I had not the essentials (vide N°. 18). There was no time to loose, for had I delayed a moment, all my time, which was several years with the closest attention, all my expences, which had been very great, to the most of all I had, would have been irrecoverably lost; besides, had I exhibited my first boat, it would have been construed into an acknowledgment of Mr. Fitch's assertion, by producing a boat with which steam had nothing to do. These considerations compelled me to pursue the perfecting my steam-engines with increased ardor, and happy am I to inform the public, they are now so far completed, as to manifest their valuable purposes for the navigations before-mentioned, applicable to vessels of all dimensions, equal to forcing boats by the assistance of poles, worked

by

by the fame machine, againſt any rapid the fame boats can with ſafety come down; and, for raiſing water, for griſt or ſaw-mills watering meadows, or purpoſes of agriculture, cheaper than races can be dug of any conſiderable diſtance, or dams made, whilſt Mr. Fitch is praying the different Aſſemblies for four years longer to perfect his *thing*, not to mention the enormous difference there is in weight, machinery and expences, between his ſteam-engine and mine, (to be ſatisfied in this particular, the reader will be pleaſed to turn to the annexed papers, Nᵒ. 6 and 7.)

Leaſt it ſhould be ſuggeſted that I borrowed my principles of Mr. Fitch (though I believe the fact to be exactly the reverſe) I have been at the pains to prove inconteſtibly, that my idea of a boat to be worked by ſteam, was a conſiderable time before his, and that my idea had been mentioned at Kentuckey, (from whence, I am told, he brought his) by a gentleman to whom I communicated it, previous to his departure for that country. For the former, the reader will be pleaſed to refer to the annexed affidavits, Nᵒ. 8, 9, 10, 11, 12, and to a paragraph from his Excellency General Waſhington's letter, in anſwer to mine, of the tenth of March, 1785, Nᵒ. 13, and to Govenor Johnſon's letter, Nᵒ. 14, for the latter (that is, of my intentions being mentioned at Kentuckey,) to Mr. Michael Bedinger's affidavit, No. 15.

I have been unavoidably led to mention Mr. Fitch for my own juſtification, and to prove my prior right to the ſteam invention, and I ſhould have ſaid no more, but let experience determine whoſe principles are foundeſt, had not Mr. Fitch, equally void of decency and truth, aſſerted "I got what ſmall knowledge I have of ſteam boats from him." Nᵒ. 18. By the reſpectable teſtimony of his Excellency General Waſhington, Nᵒ. 13; by Governor Johnſon, No. 14, and by certificates and affidavits of many other gentlemen, hereunto annexed, I prove my idea was nearly maturated, before ſteam had ever entered his imagination, by his own confeſſion to Governor Johnſon; nor was my priority unknown to Mr. Fitch, for General Waſhington informed him, " though he thought himſelf not at liberty to diſcloſe my principles, yet he would aſſure him his thought was not original, and that I had mentioned the application of ſteam to him before," (No. 14) and therefore he declined giving Mr. Fitch an introductory letter to the Aſſembly of Virginia. What dependence can the public put in the promiſes of a man, who has knowingly and unprovokedly (for I never ſaw Mr. Fitch) treated an individual ſo unworthily. Now I can, with truth aſſure the public, that Mr. Fitch's boat, ſo loaded with machinery, complexity and expence, (granting his machine all the properties he aſcribed to it in his publication) can never be uſeful; becauſe, his powers, by his own ſhewing, allowing for frictions and the neceſſary flipping of his paddles through the water, will

will not propel his boat, at the rate of more than *three* miles in an hour, where no current opposes.

If Mr. Fitch did get his first idea of a steam boat, from what Captain Bedinger said respecting mine, at Kentuckey, (which circumstances leave little room to doubt) and thought himself justified in making an application to his own advantage, as it was not delivered to him in confidence, surely nothing can be said in his defence, for endeavouring to rob the first inventor of his right, and, by changing persons with him, to transfer the odium of plagiarism from himself to the real proprietor.

But it is astonishing what latitude some men will give themselves, for the wickedness of a certain —— ——, is, I think, without parallel. In or about the month of June, 1787, this Mr. —— informed me he had invented a machine to raise water, by the action of that water alone; that he was preparing a number of wheels, and other things for perfecting his machine, and begged to know my opinion of it; at the same time making the utmost professions of secrecy and friendship. To save him the expence of preparing materials for a machine, which must, from the nature of things, prove abortive, without enquiring into his plan, I convinced him, by explaining great part of mine, of the impossibility of his success. Having, by his professions, and all outward shews of religion gained so much of my confidence and secret, he soon after removed himself to Baltimore, where he caused a machine to be made on the out-work of my principles (though very imperfect, for he was not entrusted with some of the most material parts) which he exhibited to view, and had the audacity to petition the Maryland Assembly to give him an exclusive right for the emoluments of another's invention, so surreptitiously obtained; but he received the denial he so justly merited. The reader will be pleased to peruse Nᵒ· 16 and 17, hereunto annexed, for the whole of this pitiful transaction.

The following EXPLANATION will give a general idea of the principles by which *steam* acts on my boat. Accurate calculations of the particular powers, seem not necessary here to be given.

In the bottom of the boat, where a kelson should be, there is a trunk 36 feet long; the after end is open, and terminates at the stern post; the other end is closed, and the whole trunk, according to its dimensions, occupies about three-fourth parts of the length of the boat. On the closed end of this trunk stands a cylinder, two and a half feet long, from this cylinder there is a communication into the trunk, which lets water pass freely from the cylinder to the trunk, through which it is discharged by the stern. There is another communication from the bottom of the cylinder, by a tube or pipe, to the river or water under the

the boat; on the top of this tube, and within the cylinder, there is a valve to admit the water from the river into the cylinder; it likewise prevents it from returning again the same way. On the top of this cylinder there stands another of the same length, and is fixed to the under one by screws; each of these cylinders have a piston made tight, which work up and down with very little friction; these pistons are connected with each other by a smooth bolt, (they being well screwed to its ends) passing through the bottom of the upper cylinder; the lower cylinder acts as a pump, which draws water from the river through the tube and valve before described; the return of the piston forces it through the trunk before-mentioned, and out near the stern of the boat. The upper cylinder acts as a steam-engine, and receives its steam from a boiler under its piston, which piston is then carried up to the top of the cylinder by the steam; at the same time, the piston of the lower cylinder is brought up to its top, from its connection with the upper piston, by the aforesaid bolt; at which time they shut up the communication from the boiler, and open another to discharge the steam for condensation; by this means the atmosphere acts upon the piston of the upper cylinder, and its force is conveyed to the piston in the lower cylinder, by the aforesaid connecting bolt; which forces the water, then in the lower cylinder, through the trunk, with considerable velocity; the re-action whereof, on the other end of the trunk, is the power which drives the boat forward.

To prove the Use of the Trunk.

IT is well known that any heavy body falling near the earth, will pass through a space of about fifteen feet in the first second of time; if the same body was acted upon in a horizontal direction, by an impulse equal to its weight, it would move in that direction the same distance in an equal time; it follows then, that the water in the trunk, will have the effect proportionable to its weight, of retarding the water from being discharged from the cylinder in too short a time; to prevent the water, which after the stroke, moves rapidly out of the trunk, from retarding the forward motion of the boat, by its velocity.

There is a valve near the cylinder, on the top of the trunk, to admit air, which follows the water that is in motion, and gives time for the water to rise gradually into the trunk through valves, at its bottom, for that purpose; this water has little or no motion with respect to the boat, and is therefore capable of resisting the next stroke of the engine.

Thus I have laid the principles of my boat before the public, and can assure them, by the wonderful force of steam, issuing in incredible quantities, from an entirely new constructed boiler, no doubt remains, but all the advantages which I have before-
mentioned,

mentioned, both with refpect to navigation and the raifing of water, will be produced. The one I have actually proved, by a loaded boat being propelled againft a ftream with the velocity of four miles in an hour, in the prefence and to the great fatisfaction of numerous fpectators, and the other by models now ready to be produced, which admit not of contradiction.

If the public think thefe inventions, which muft be productive of the greateft ufefulnefs, worthy their patronage, I cannot fear but an exclufive right will be granted me by the different Affemblies of the United States, for a given number of years, which they fhall think right, for the erecting thefe machines of my own invention, to compenfate me for the trouble, for the time, for the expence and for the fatigue which they have coft me.

If a committee of experimental philofophers fhould be appointed in each ftate, to examine me, it would give me infinite pleafure to attend, and convince them of the practicability of all I have propofed; of the fimplicity of my machines, and of the fmallnefs of their expence.

I am with great refpect,

the Public's moft devoted,

and obedient humble fervant,

JAMES RUMSEY.

Berkeley County, Virginia, January 1, 1788.

Berkeley County, ſſ.

WE, the fubfcribers, Juftices of the Peace for the county aforefaid, do certify, that the annexed affidavits, certificates and extracts of letters have been examined by us, and are true copies from the originals.

JOHN KEARSLEY,

December 28, 1787. CATO MOORE.

Virginia, Berkeley County, ſſ.

I, MOSES HUNTER, Clerk of the faid county, do hereby certify, that John Kearfley and Cato Moore, Gentlemen, who have fubfcribed the above certificate, were at that time, and ftill are, Juftices of the Peace for faid county, and that all due faith and credit is and ought to be given to all probates by them fo figned, as well in Juftice Courts as thereout. In teftimony whereof, I have hereunto fet my hand, and affixed the feal of the faid county, this 29th. day of December, 1787.

MOSES HUNTER.

C. F. R.

CERTIFICATES, &c.

No. 1.

Berkeley County, Vir. ff.

ON Monday, December 3, 1787, I was requested to fee an experiment on Potowmack river, made by Mr. James Rumsey's Steam Boat, and had no fmall pleafure to fee her get on her way, with near half her burthen on board, and move againft the current at the rate of three miles per hour, -by the force of fteam, without any external application whatever. I am well informed, and verily believe, that the machine at prefent is very imperfect, and by no means capable of performing what it would do if completed: I have not the leaft doubt but it may be brought into common and beneficial ufe, and be of advantage to all navigations, as the machine is fimple, light and cheap, and will be exceedingly durable, and does not occupy a fpace in the boat of more than four feet by two and a half.

HORATIA GATES,
Late Major General in the Continental Army.

No. 2.

Berkeley County, Vir. ff.

On Monday, December 3, 1787, I was requefted to fee an experiment on Potowmack river, made by Mr. James Rumsey's Steam Boat, and had no fmall pleafure to fee her get under way with near half her burthen on board, and move againft the current at the rate of three miles per hour, by the force of fteam, without any external application whatever: I am well informed, and do verily believe, that the machine at prefent is very imperfect, and by no means capable of performing what it would do if completed: I have not the leaft doubt but it may be brought into common and beneficial ufe, and be of great advantage to all navigations, as the machine is fimple, light and cheap, and will be exceedingly durable, and does not occupy a fpace in the boat more than four feet by two and a half.

ROBERT STUBBS,
Teacher of the Academy in Shepherd's-Town.

Berkeley County, Vir. ff.

The Rev. Robert Stubbs, Gent. Teacher of the Academy at Shepherd's-Town, acknowledged before us, magiftrates for faid county, that he did fubfcribe the above writing.

Given under our hands, 14th. Dec. 1787.

CATO MOORE,
JOHN KEARSLEY.

No. 3.

No. 3.

Berkeley County, Vir. ff.

Being requested to see an experiment made by Mr. JAMES RUMSEY's Steam Boat, on Potowmack river, on Monday, the 3d. of December, 1787, it was with great pleasure that we saw her get under way, with two tons on board, exclusive of her machinery, and move against the current at the rate of three miles an hour, by the force of steam, without any external application whatever: We are well informed, and believe, that the machinery at present is very imperfect, and by no means capable of performing what it would do if completed. We are persuaded it may be brought into common and beneficial use, and be of great advantage to all navigations, as the machine is simple, light and cheap, and does not occupy a space in the boat of more than four feet by two and a half.

ABRAHAM SHEPHERD,	JOHN MORROW,
WILLIAM BRICE,	HENRY BEDINGER,
DAVID GRAY,	THOMAS WHITE.
CHARLES MORROW,	

Berkeley County, Vir. ff.

Personally appeared before us, John Kearsley and Cato Moore, Justices of the Peace for the county aforesaid, the sundry subscribers to the above certificate, who are all gentlemen of reputation, and by us supposed to be competent judges of what they have set forth, and they acknowledge the same to be their voluntary act; we were likewise present at the exhibition, and certify the truth of the above certificate.

Given under our hands this 13th. of December, 1787.

JOHN KEARSLEY,
CATO MOORE.

No. 4.

Berkeley County, Vir. ff.

Being requested to attend an experiment made by Mr. JAMES RUMSEY with his Steam Boat, on Potowmack river, on Tuesday the 11th. day of December, 1787, it was with great pleasure we saw her advance against the current, with about three tons on board, at the rate of four miles an hour, without an oar, or any thing but the force of steam, either to generate or assist the motion—if the machinery had been in good order, we have reason to believe, she would have gone much faster; and as the machine is light and cheap, we are well persuaded that it may be of great advantage in navigation.

MOSES HOGE,	BENENI SWEARINGEN,
CORNEL. WYNKOOP,	JOHN MORROW,
JOHN MARK,	JOS. SWEARING.
	N. B.

B

N. B. We think the machinery does not weigh more than fix or feven hundred weight, and is not included in the burthen mentioned above.

Berkeley County, Vir. ſſ.

Perſonally appeared before us, two of the Juſtices of the Peace for the county aforeſaid, the ſundry ſubſcribers to the above certificate, who are all gentlemen of reputation, and by us ſuppoſed to be competent judges of what they have ſet forth; and they acknowledge the ſame to be their voluntary act. December 13th. 1787.

CATO MOORE,
JOHN KEARSLEY.

Nᶜ· 5.

Berkeley County, Vir. ſſ.

Being requeſted to ſee an experiment made by Mr. JAMES RUMSEY's Steam Boat, on Potowmack river, on Thurſday the 11th. of December, 1787, it was with great pleaſure that we ſaw her get under way, with upwards of three tons on board, and move againſt the current at the rate of four miles an hour, by the force of ſteam, without any external application whatever: We are well informed, and believe, that the machinery at preſent is very imperfect, and by no means capable of performing what it would do if completed; we are perſuaded that it may be brought into common and beneficial uſe, and be of great advantage to navigation, as the machine is ſimple, light and cheap, and does not occupy a ſpace of more than four feet by two and a half.

CHARLES MORROW, ABRA. SHEPHERD,
THOMAS WHITE, HENRY BEDINGER.
ROBERT STUBBS,

Berkeley County, Vir. ſſ.

Perſonally appeared before us, two of the Juſtices of the Peace for the county aforeſaid, the ſundry ſubſcribers to the above certificate, who are all gentlemen of reputation, and by us ſuppoſed to be competent judges of what they have ſet forth, and they acknowledge the ſame to be their voluntary act.

Given under our hands, this 14th. December, 1787.

CATO MOORE,
JOHN KEARSLEY·

Nᵒ· 6.

Berkeley County, Vir. ſſ.

The Affidavit of WILLIAM ASKEW, of Berkeley county, and ſtate of Virginia, ſheweth, That he was in the city of Philadelphia, as well as he remembers, in the month of September laſt, when he had an opportunity of ſeeing what is called the Steam-
Boat

Boat, said to be constructed by Mr. FITCH; on taking a view
of which boat, (and from the information of a gentleman, who
appeared to be concerned in the said machine) this deponent is
of opinion, that the boiler will hold five hundred gallons of
water. From what he was informed, by the gentleman aforesaid, and from his own view, his opinion is, that the machinery
of Mr. FITCH's Boat, on a moderate calculation, will, on its
present construction weigh seven tons, exclusive of the quantity
of wood necessary for the boiler. This deponent further saith,
that he verily believes the machinery of Mr. FITCH's steam-boat
must necessarily cost three hundred pounds.—This deponent hath
lately seen the steam-boat constructed by Mr. JAMES RUMSEY,
of Berkeley county, Virginia, and believes from good information, as well as his own opinion on examination, that Mr.
RUMSEY's steam machinery will not, on its present construction,
weigh more than eight hundred pounds and may be worked with
a very inconsiderable quantity of wood, or coals, perhaps not
more coals in twelve hours that four bushels; and that Mr.
RUMSEY's boiler need have no more water, at one time, than
one pint, or perhaps not so much, to keep the machinery in
sufficient motion to stem the stream of a river, sufficiently fast
to be safe with a cargo of goods. This deponent is well convinced that the whole of Mr. RUMSEY's machinery may be
made for twenty pounds, nor will it occupy more room in a
boat that four barrels of flour.

Berkeley County, Vir. ss.
This day Mr. WILLIAM ASKEW came before me, and made
oath, that the above testimony as far as came within his own
knowledge, is true, and so he believes is the information he received from others. Sworn before me, December 8th. 1787.
JAMES WILSON.

N°. 7.
Berkeley County, Vir. ss.
TO WHOM IT MAY CONCERN,
On application of Mr. JAMES RUMSEY and sundry other gentlemen, requesting my opinion, whether Mr. FITCH's or Mr.
RUMSEY's Steam Boat, agreeably to the present different plans
of working each boat, would be of the greatest public utility;
I have, at their importunities, consented, (as far as my knowledge of the matter will admit) to give my opinion, without re-
serve, to the best of my judgment; and, as I have seen both Mr.
FITCH's and Mr. RUMSEY's steam-boats, with the machinery,
or at least so much thereof as could be observed, by a common
examination, I presume that Mr. RUMSEY's plan is much the
most elegible, simple and practicable. Mr. FITCH's machinery
appears bulky, weighty and complicated, leaving little room in
the boat in which I saw it for loading. The weight of the whole
apparatus

apparatus I fuppofe to be five tons—whereas the whole of Mr. Rumsey's machinery, at the time of exhibiting publicly, with every apparatus complete, could not weigh more than five hundred pounds.

It is obvious, therefore, that a machine weighing one twentieth only, and of fmall fize, comparative with the other, and by many degrees lefs complicated, muft prove of the greateft public utility, and will be practifed in preference to the other.

I do therefore give it as my opinion, that Mr. Rumsey's plan is to be preferred to Mr. Fitch's.

Given under my hand, at Shepherd's-Town, this 6th. day of December, 1787.

HENRY BEDINGER,

Berkeley County, Vir. ff.

Captain Henry Bedinger acknowledged before us, Magiftrates for the faid county, that he fubfcribed the above writing.

Given under our hands, this 14th. day of Dec. 1787.

CATO MOORE,
JOHN KEARSLEY,

Berkeley County, Vir. ff.

We, the fubfcribers, have been long acquainted with the within mentioned Capt. HENRY BEDINGER, and have ever found him a worthy honeft gentleman.

HORATIA GATES,   CHARLES MORROW,
THOMAS WHITE,   JOHN MARK,
JOHN MORROW,   ROBERT STUBBS,
BENONI SWEARINGEN, JOS. SWEARINGEN,
ABRAHAM SHEPHERD,   JOHN KEARSLEY.

December 14, 1787.

Berkeley County, Vir. ff.

The above gentlemen, who are all of good fame, fubfcribed the above certificate in my prefence. Given under my hand, this 14th. December, 1787.

CATO MOORE.

Nᵒ. 8.

Berkeley County, Vir. ff.

This day came GEORGE ROOTES, before me, one of the Juftices of the Peace for the county aforefaid, and made oath, that Mr. JAMES RUMSEY informed him, in the year 1784, that he was projecting a boat to work with fteam, and the faid George has heard, and verily believes, that the faid Mr. RUMSEY, from the time of his leaving the agency of the Potowmack Company, has purfued his intention of perfecting his fteam-engine for that purpofe with unremitted attention, which the faid George is informed is now in great forwardnefs. Given under my hand, this 24th. day of November, 1787.

WILLIAM LITTLE,

Nᵒ. 9.

No. 9.

Berkeley County, Vir. ff.

This day came Mr. CHARLES MORROW, before me, one of the Justices of the Peace for the said county, and made oath, that in the beginning of the year 1785, Mr. JAMES RUMSEY told him, that by making use of steam he could raise WATER for MILLS, and that he would do it as soon as he had completed his steam-boat.

CHARLES MORROW.

Sworn to, and subscribed before me, this 13th of December, 1787.

JOHN KEARSLEY.

No. 10.

Berkeley County, Vir. ff.

This day came NICHOLAS ORRICK, before me, one of the Justices of the Peace for the county aforesaid, and made oath, that Mr. JAMES RUMSEY informed him, in the year 1784, that he was projecting a boat to work with steam, and that he the said Nicholas doth know that the said Mr. RUMSEY from that time has pursued his intention of perfecting his steam-engine for that purpose, and the said Nicholas has been on board of the said RUMSEY's boat, when going by the power of steam, and has reason to believe it may answer a valuable purpose when completed. Given under my hand, this 24th. day of November, 1787.

WILLIAM LITTLE.

No. 11.

Berkeley County, Vir. ff.

This day came CHARLES MORROW, before me, one of the Justices of the Peace for the aforesaid county, and made oath, that in the course of the summer 1785, Mr. JAMES RUMSEY had a boat built near the town of Bath; that early in the fall he had her brought down the river to Shepherd's-Town, and shortly after Mr. JOSEPH BARNS was sent to Baltimore, in order to have some machinery cast; that he then understood the boat was to be propelled by steam; that shortly after Mr. BARNS returned from Baltimore he was sent to Frederick-Town, in order to have some other things made, agreeable to Mr. RUMSEY's directions, and thinks he returned from thence about the middle of November; that the said Charles then saw the machinery Mr. BARNS had got made, viz. a boiler, two cylenders, pumps, pipes, &c. That about the first of December it appeared to the said Charles, that the whole of the machinery was ready to be fixed to the boat, which came down to the Falls of Shanadoah for experiment, but the ice then commencing prevented it for the winter.

That

That in the winter Mr. Rumsey told him he had made fundry improvements; in particular, that he had invented an entirely new conftructed boiler; that the faid Rumfey fent to a forge for iron, and fet two fmiths to work, with directions how to make it; but when it was ready to be put together, he found, upon examination, that the workmanfhip was fo badly executed, that it would not anfwer the purpofe; he therefore concluded to try an experiment with his old boiler; and the faid Charles fays, that Mr. Barns (Mr. Rumfey's principal mechanic) continued during the winter to execute the different improvements Mr. Rumsey had made; in the fpring, 1786, the machinery was put on the boat, and the firft trial made, the faid Charles being on board; that fhe went againft the current until the fteam efcaped, by the then imperfectnefs of the machine. Upon an experiment made with the new boiler, the heat of the fteam was fo greatly increafed, that it diffolved the foft folder, which had been thought, and before had proved, fufficient for cementing the fundry parts of fuch machines; and as hard folder was obliged to be ufed in the repairs, delays were neceffarily created. July, 1787, Mr. Rumfey had his new conftructed boiler repaired, which he, the faid Charles, conceives to be the moft capital con- trivance to make fteam that can be invented; for when the ma- chine is not at work, the whiftling of the fteam may be heard at leaft half a mile; and he is convinced that it does not hold more than three gallons of water; and the faid Charles further faith, that Mr. Rumfey has for feveral years fteadily purfued his boat fcheme, to the total neglect of every other kind of bufinefs which has very confiderably injured his circumftances, having Mr. Barns employed at five pounds per month, fince the year eighty- five; and that he conceives the boat to be now near her comple- tion: And the faid Charles has not a doubt but Mr. Rumfey is equal to the tafk of making her perform according to his original pofition.

CHARLES MORROW.
Sworn to and fubfcribed before me, December 8th. 1787.
JOHN KEARSLEY.

Nº. 12.

Berkeley County, Vir. ff.

This day came Jofeph Barns before me, one of the Juftices of the Peace for the faid county, and made oath, that he was employed by Mr. James Rumfey, in May, 1785, to build a boat on Potowmack river, near the town of Bath, and that he was then informed by the faid Rumfey, that the boat, when finifhed, was to be propelled by fteam, and that he had built the boat foon after (he thinks in September) he went, by the requeft of Mr. Rumfey, to Baltimore, to get fome machinary caft for the boat; and in October and November, in Frederick town, he

got,

got, all the other machinery made for an experiment by steam: In December it was put on the boat, at Shanandoah Falls, but before it could be got ready for trial, the ice began to drive, which prevented it: Also, that Mr. Rumsey, during the winter, invented his new constructed boiler, and had it made ready to put together before the spring, but it was so badly executed, that he declined making the experiment with it, but proposed to try his old boiler: Accordingly, in April, 1786, the experiment was made, and the boat went against the current of Potowmack; but many parts of the machine being imperfect, and and some parts rendered useless by the heat of the steam, he was obliged to have it repaired, which was done at the Great Falls, and she was again tried, but failed in the repaired work, though it made many powerful strokes before it failed, and sent the boat forward with such power, that one man was not able to hold her. The next experiment was attempted in December, with the new constructed boiler, but the violence of the heat was so great, from the steam, that it melted the soft solder that great part of the machine was put together with, and rendered it entirely useless, until repaired with hard solder; about this time, the ice drifting, carried off the boat which the machinery was made for, and destroyed her in such a manner, that the repairing her was equal to one half the expence of building a new one: That the boat was, in the Spring, 1787, repaired, the machine also, and was ready for trial in September, when the boat moved up the river, against the current, with about two tons on board, besides the machine, at the rate of two miles per hour; but the new boiler was so badly made, that it opened at several of its joints, which let great quantities of the steam escape: And the said Barns further saith, that to his knowledge, the machine at the last trial, on December 3, 1787, was very imperfect in many parts, as the same boiler was then made use of, after receiving some repairs: It is his opinion it may be brought to answer very valuable purposes, as it will be simple, cheap, light, and durable, and may be applied to a ship of the largest size to advantage, having no external application whatever: And the said Barns further saith, that Mr. Rumsey has, to his knowledge, injured his circumstances very much, by quitting all kinds of business to pursue the boat; that he, the said Barns, has received of the said Mr. Rumsey five pounds per month, besides his board, from April, 1785, to the present time; which, in his opinion, is but a small part of the expences the said Mr. Rumsey must have been at in the prosecuting his plan. His new constructed boiler must exceed every thing of that kind yet extant, as it will not hold more than twenty pints, and, in his opinion, will make more steam than a five hundred gallon boiler in the common way; and from the observation he has made, has reason to believe, that six bushels of good coals will serve it for twelve hours.

The

The weight of the prefent machine is about feven hundred pounds, and will not occupy more fpace than four barrels.

Sworn before me, this 10th. December, 1787.

CATO MOORE.

N⁰· 13.

A PARAGRAPH from General Washington's Letter, in anfwer to mine of the 10th. of March, 1785.

" It gives me much pleafure to find by your letter, that you are not lefs fanguine in your Boat project than when I faw you in Richmond, and that you have made fuch further difco-veries as will render them more extenfively ufeful than was at firft expected. You have my beft wifhes for the fuccefs of your plan."

N⁰· 14.

Annapolis, December 18, 1787.

Sir,

In compliance with your requeft, I mention the principle facts and circumftances with which I am acquainted refpecting your Steam Engine, and your expectation of its effect in boat vaviga-tion. I was entirely ignorant of the principle on which you were to gain your power, and your manner of applying it, till our return from the Great Falls together, in October or November, (but I think in October) 1785, when you told me that you relied on fteam for your firft power, and wifhed me to promote you, having cylenders caft at my brother's and my works; the attempt did not fucceed—I confidered myfelf under an obligation to fe-crecy till in the progrefs of making copper cylenders in Frede-rick-town fome time after, when I found, that the defigned pur-pofe of the cylender was a fubject of pretty general converfa-tion.

Being on the committee appointed to confider and report on Mr. Fitch's petition, I thought it my duty to mention what was in my memory, of your telling me of your having communicated your principle to General Wafhington, as I thought, though perhaps miftakenly, at the time your model and experiment were exhibited before the General; and, with the approbation of the committee, wrote to the General on the fubject: His anfwer, now before me, is to the effect, that " At that time, September 1784, nothing was intimated of fteam: That the November following, in Richmond, you fpoke to him of the effect of fteam, and of the conviction you were under of the ufefulnefs of its applicati-on for the purpofe of inland navigation," but the General feems to have thought it an immatured idea, that he did not then ima-gine you relied on.

Mr. Fitch having often mentioned the time (I think April, 1785) when the idea firft ftruck him, and yours being prior, the

committee

committee could not report in favour of Mr. Fitch. The Gen.
added in his anfwer, " It is proper for me herewith to add,
that fome time after this Mr. Fitch called on me, in his way to
Richmond, and explaining his fcheme, wanted a letter from me
introductory to the Affembly of this (Virginia) ftate; the giving
of which I declined, and went fo far as to inform him, that tho'
I was enjoined not to difclofe the principles of Mr. Rumfey's
difcovery, yet, would venture to affure him, that he thought of
applying fteam was not original, but had been mentioned to me
by Mr. Rumfey."

I efteem myfelf no way competent to decide on Philofophical or mechanical principles, but if you can fimplify the fteam-
engine, render it cheap, and apply its powers to raife water in
great quantities, for the purpofes of agriculture and water-works
of all kinds, or apply the powers more immediately, as has
been much the fubject of converfation between us at times, every man may eafily perceive a vaft field of improvement will
thereby be opened, which I moft fincerely wifh you may largely
reap the good fruits of.

I am, Sir, your moft obedient fervent,

THOMAS JOHNSON.

N°. 15.

Berkeley County, Vir. ff.

This day came Michael Bedinger, before me, one of the juftices of the Peace for the faid county, and made oath, that Mr.
James Rumfey informed him, in, or before the month of March,
1784, that he was of opinion that a boat might be conftructed
to work by fteam, and that he intended to give it a trial, and
mentioned fome of the machinery that would be neceffary to
reduce it to practice; And the faid Michael further faith, that he
fet out for Kentuckey country immediately after in order to fur-
vey fome lands, and refided there upwards of eighteen months,
and that during the time of his ftay there, he frequently mentioned Mr. Rumfery's boat fcheme: He believes that he alfo
mentioned, that it was to be wrought by fteam.

The above was voluntarily fworn to before me, by Captain
Bedinger, who is a gentleman of reputation.

November 28, 1787.

JOHN KEARSLEY.

We, whofe names are hereunto fubfcribed, certify, that the
within mentioned Michael Bedinger is a gentleman of reputation and veracity.

HORATIA GATES,	CHARLES MORROW,
THOMAS WHITE,	JOHN MARK,
JAMES KERNEY,	PHIL. PENDLETON,
JOHN MORROW,	ROBERT STUBBS.
JOSEPH MITCHEL	

C

N°. 16.

Berkeley County, Vir. ſſ.
TO WHOM IT MAY CONCERN.

I, Charles Morrow, of Shepherd's-Town, Berkeley county, commonwealth of Virginia, do certify, that late in the ſpring or beginning of ſummer, 1787, a certain —— ——, of Baltimore Town, formerly of this place, called at my houſe, when the converſation turned on Mr. Rumſey's Steam Boat and mechanical powers; he then told me, that before he had converſed with Mr. Rumſey, he conceived he new a great deal of theſe matters; but he now found he knew very little, and ſaid, " I muſt give up to Mr. Rumſey, he is my maſter." The truth of which ſhould Mr. —— deny (which I hardly think he will) I will at any time declare on oath. I do further certify, that Mr. Enoch Martin, of this county, informed me, that on Sunday, the 18th inſtant, he ſaw, in miniature, an engine at work in Baltimore town, which Mr. —— had made to raiſe water by ſteam; and that the ſaid —— told him he received the firſt inſight of that matter from Mr. Rumſey.

Given under my hand, this 13th December, 1787.
CHARLES MORROW.
Teſt.
DAVID GRAY,
JOSEPH BARNS.

Berkeley County, Vir. ſſ.
This day came Joſeph Barns before me, one of the Juſtices of the peace for the ſaid county, and made oath, that Mr. James Rumſey informed him, the year 1785, that he had contrived a very ſimple, cheap machine, to raiſe water by ſteam and the power of the atmoſphere. That ſome time (he thinks) in the month of June, 1787, a certain —— ——, of Baltimore-Town, formerly of Shepherd's-Town, did by ſome means, though it was not cuſtomary, inſinuate himſelf ſo as to be ſeveral times admitted into the ſhop where the ſteam-engine for the boat was making, and then almoſt finiſhed; and the ſaid Barns further ſaith, he heard Mr. Rumſey inform the ſaid —— of his intention of raiſing water by ſteam, to work mills, as ſoon as he had accompliſhed his boat ſcheme, and then proceeded to explain to the ſaid —— the principles by which water might be raiſed, and alſo explained ſundry parts of the machinery, he believes all, except ſome valves and the opening and ſhutting of cocks by the machinery at the proper times; and the ſaid Barns well remembers, that during Mr. Rumſey's explanations, the ſaid —— ſeemed much aſtoniſhed, and declared that he never knew till then that the atmoſphere had any weight, or that ſteam had

liad fuch power; and that he then clearly faw the reafon that a machine he had fome time before invented to raife water, would not anfwer the purpofe; and that it was fo foolifh a plan, he faid, he was afhamed to explain it, And the faid Barns further faith, that Mr. Rumfey gave the faid —— a copy of his calculations of the force and velocity of water from under different heads, which he informed the faid —— would enable him to fee the propriety of his calculations for raifing water, by which he might eftimate the quantity neceffary to work a mill.

Berkeley County, Vir. ff.

The above-mentioned Jofeph Barns came perfonally before me, a magiftrate for the faid county, and made oath, that the above writing contained the truth, and that there was an exact copy of the annexed calculation delivered to —— ——, by Mr. James Rumfey. Given under my hand, this 14th. day of Dec. 1787.
CATO MOORE.

We, the fubfcribers, have been long acquainted with Mr. Jofeph Barns, and ever found him to be a worthy honeft man, and a man of truth.

ROBERT STUBBS,	CHARLES MORROW,
HEN. BEDINGER,	BENENI SWEARINGEN,
ABRA. SHEPHERD,	CORNEL WYNCOOP,
JOHN MARK,	THOMAS WHITE,
JOHN MORROW,	JOS. SWEARINGEN.

Berkeley County, Vir. ff.

The above gentlemen, who are all of good fame, fubfcribed the above certificate in my prefence.
CATO MOORE.

⁎⁎ The calculations alluded to in this affidavit were at firft intended to be printed, its length determined the author to decline it—if —— fhould deny he had fuch a copy, it will be produced for the fatisfaction of the public.

Nᵒ· 18.

The underwritten is a paragraph of a letter written from a Mr. Daniel Buckley, living near Philadelphia, to a gentleman of Berkeley county, Virginia, and " Dr. McMahon," who Mr. Buckley is fo concerned for, is a partner with Mr. Rumfey in his fteam-boat. 'Tis copied and annexed to prove how bufy Mr. Fitch has been in calumny, and how eafily he found credit and propagators. Should he incline to affert hereafter, what credit he will deferve has been fo clearly proved, that future impofitions may be avoided; and thofe who fpread a flander they do not believe, deferve the contempt of all honeft men.

" Pleafe

"Pleafe to give my fincere refpects to Doctor Mc Mahon and his worthy lady—he is my moft particular acquaintance, and truly I am forry he has been deluded by a perfon, who I have reafon to believe is a deceiver, as Mr. Fitch, of Philadelphia, fays, Mr. Rumfey got what fmall knowledge he had of fteam from him, but he retained the effentials, without which, he fays, Mr. Rumfey cannot fucceed."

We do certify that the above paragraph was taken from the aforefaid letter; and copied in our prefence.

GEORGE ROOTES,
CHARLES MORROW.

☞ [The perfon's name omitted in republifhing Mr. Rumfey's pamphlet; is, becaufe he has no connection with me, or my project, being a ftranger, and probably innocent of the charges alledged.]   *J. F.*

www.ingramcontent.com/pod-product-compliance
Lightning Source LLC
Chambersburg PA
CBHW030901260626
47169CB00008B/2631